REBLOOMED LOVE

LOVE THAT NEVER ENDED

THARUN K

Made with ♥ on the Notion Press Platform
www.notionpress.com

"To those who love from afar, with a heart full of dreams and a whisper of hope"

Contents

About Author

THARUN K

Tharun born on April 11, 2003 in Thirthahalli, a small town in Shivamogga district, Karnataka he spent most of his life in his hometown only. After he went to Mysuru for higher studies. Now currently studying in Bengaluru. This is first book by him. His love for book stared in the covid lockdown. He started writing book after he moved to Bengaluru.

You can reach out him at his Instagram handle @_tharun._.k

Write to him at tharunparth23@gmail.com

Foreword

All the love stories don't have a happy ending. Some have a sad ending also, but this the story which was at the stage of sad ending. But became a happy ending. The destiny played many times with their relationship. But the love between them was so strong that even destiny accepted the defeat

Preface

Some stories are beautiful when it's left incomplete. But Some are sad when it's left incomplete.

Likewise, some stories are beautiful when it's completed. But some are sad when it's completed.

This is the story which was sad when it was incomplete. But even God didn't like the sad incomplete ending. So, he decided to bloom the love again and make the story complete and happy.

The whole story is filled with the roller coaster of emotions. So, lets fasten the seatbelts and dive into the story where the love bloomed again. Let's see a saga of the story REBLOOMED LOVE

Acknowledgements

The title of the book that came to me when I was at Kodaikanal with one of my dearest friend. Thanks to the old lady who gave me knowledge about flowers when I was on a trip. The trip which I'll never forget.

The old lady selling flowers was the one who explained me that some Daylily varieties bloom more than once during a single season. Some bloom early and then again in the fall, while others have a bloom for several month.

That made me think it was pretty much like my story. So, I searched that what are those varieties called that was the time I got to know the Word Reblooming.

From there came the title of my first book "REBLOOMED LOVE"

True love happens only once, it's more beautiful when the first love will be your true love. Only some get to experience those things.

The story revolves around the boy who found a true love in his first love even the distance and destiny got defeated by the power of love.

Let's go through the story of **Partha** and **Pari.** And see their happy movements and their memories and all the tough time they went through out their life.

1

Kind of Love at First Sight...

Partha was an ordinary sixth-grade student, hailing from a humble middle-class family. He was the kind of boy who spent his days studying, playing, and indulging in the mischief typical of children his age. His life was simple—he had no big dreams or ambitions, just the usual joys of childhood. But one chilly December morning, everything changed.

That day, Partha arrived at school a little earlier than usual. The crisp air and the soft hum of the morning set the perfect backdrop as he sat in the classroom, playing with a puzzle scale—an item that was considered "illegal" for school in the early 2000s. Suddenly, the door opened, and in walked Pari, his classmate since Pre-KG. He had known her well, but that day, something was different.

She was wearing a purple and black kurthi, her hair loosely flowing around her face. The moment Partha saw her, he felt a strange flutter in his chest. It was as if the world had paused for a moment, and the cool breeze that swept through the room only made her seem even more ethereal. He couldn't explain it, but it was as if something deep inside him had awakened. The way Shah Rukh Khan once said, "Agar kisi cheez ko dil se chaaho, toh puri khayenat usey tumse milane ki koshish mein lag jaati hai"—if you truly desire something from the depths of your heart, the whole universe will conspire to bring it to you.

"Hi, Pari," she greeted him, her voice calm and soothing.

"Hello," Partha managed to reply, his voice barely above a whisper.

From that moment on, Partha began to see Pari in a different light. What had once been a simple friendship now felt like something more, something pure and beautiful. He didn't understand it, but he knew that he wanted to be with her.

Some might argue that Partha, being just a small boy, couldn't possibly understand love. But to him, love was something simple and pure. He didn't know anything about the complexities of relationships or societal expectations. All he knew was that he wanted to make her happy, spend time with her, and share everything with her. He was ready to face any consequence, no matter how small, to be by her side.

Later that day, during the school assembly, Partha tried to stand near her. But his height was a disadvantage, and as luck would have it, the PT teacher came along and dragged him to the back of the line. Partha sighed, wishing he could talk to her, but the distance between them made it impossible.

The day continued, and as always, the first period was Hindi—a subject that Partha struggled with. The Hindi teacher was strict, and Partha often found himself on the receiving end of her scolding. On that day, he hadn't completed his homework, and as the teacher asked for the assignments, Partha knew he was in trouble. He and six other students were the only ones who hadn't submitted their work.

"I will not beat anyone today," the teacher announced, and for a moment, Partha felt a sense of relief. But then came the next words: "Anyone who didn't do their homework, get out of the class!"

Partha, though not afraid of punishment, felt humiliated. He had been hoping to impress Pari, but now, in front of everyone, he had been scolded and sent out of the class. His heart sank. He sat outside, feeling embarrassed and defeated.

During the break, Partha sat alone, his thoughts consumed by the incident. He was lost in his own world when a familiar voice broke through his thoughts.

"Are you not coming out?" Pari asked, her tone gentle.

"No," Partha replied, not realizing at first that it was Pari speaking. When he looked up and saw her standing there, his face flushed with embarrassment.

"Don't be sad, chill. It happens to everyone. Just don't do it again," Pari said with a reassuring smile.

Her kindness touched him deeply. While no one else had comforted him, Pari had. And in that moment, Partha's feelings for her grew even stronger. He realized that he wanted to be someone who could make her smile, someone worthy of her attention.

From that day forward, Partha began to change. He started completing his homework, paying attention in class, and doing his best to be a better student. His parents noticed the change in him, but they didn't question it. All that mattered to Partha was being better for Pari.

At school, students were divided into houses—Red, Yellow, Blue, and Green. Partha was in the Yellow house, and Pari was in the Green house. Every Saturday, there were no classes, just mass PT followed by group activities like singing, dancing, and clay modelling. The competition between Yellow and Green was fierce, with both houses having the most active students. Partha, however, didn't want to compete against Pari. He wanted her to win, so he began stepping back during the activities, much to the confusion of his friends, especially Anni, who had been his best friend since second grade.

"What's going on with you?" Anni asked one day. "You used to fight for the group, but now you're backing off."

"I've just lost interest," Partha replied, though he knew it wasn't true.

"I don't believe you," Anni said, skeptical. "Come on, let's talk."

Later that day, the two of them sat in Anni's balcony, sipping on cold drinks as Partha finally confessed his feelings.

"I think I have a huge crush on Pari," he admitted, his voice soft.

"You think?" Anni teased. "What do you mean, 'think'?"

"I don't know," Partha said, feeling unsure of his own feelings. "Every time I see her, I feel something I've never felt before. I just want to be with her, talk to her, and hold her hand. Even if we're just sitting together doing nothing, I feel complete."

Anni smiled. "Don't worry, I'll help you."

With Anni's support, Partha started finding ways to talk to Pari more. But confessing his feelings was still a challenge. He didn't have the courage to say the words out loud. Days turned into weeks, and Partha's longing only grew stronger.

Then came the day when the seating arrangements were changed. Partha had been trying to sit next to Pari for weeks, but his height was always an obstacle. This time, he decided to fake a vision problem, hoping to get a seat closer to her. He started making mistakes in his notes and squinting at the board, hoping the teacher would notice. But when the teacher finally did, she moved him to the front row—farther from Pari.

However, fate was on his side. The student sitting next to Pari complained about not being able to see the board, and the teacher moved him to the back, placing Partha beside Pari. He couldn't believe his luck. That afternoon, he couldn't wait to tell Anni the good news.

"Guess what?" Anni said as they met at the playground. "You're sitting next to Pari now!"

Partha couldn't contain his excitement. He hugged Anni and danced around in joy. "This calls for a treat!" he declared.

The two friends went to a bakery, celebrating with puffs and ice cream. As they left, they ran into Pari, who was out shopping with her mother.

"Hi," Pari said with a smile.

"Hello," Partha replied, his heart racing. The brief exchange felt like a dream, and Partha was left feeling as if the universe had conspired to bring him closer to her.

The next day, Partha woke up early, filled with excitement. He spent an hour getting ready, polishing his shoes, and riding his bicycle to school. He sat in his new seat, eagerly waiting for Pari to arrive. When she walked in, dressed in a red kurthi with butterflies and black denim, her beauty took his breath away.

She greeted him with a smile. "Hi, Partha! You're sitting beside me now."

Partha, though he already knew this, feigned surprise. "Oh, is it?"

As he sat down beside her, he felt a sense of peace. They exchanged a few words, and Pari asked why he had been absent the previous day. Partha, too shy to tell her the real reason, lied and said he had a stomach ache. Pari's concern for him made his heart swell.

"I'm feeling better now," he said, smiling.

The day passed in a blur, and Partha couldn't help but feel that everything was falling into place. As he helped a fellow student who had fainted during the prayer, he realized that, for the first time, he was truly happy. He was sitting beside the girl he liked, and even though it was just the beginning, it felt like everything he had ever wanted.

2
Stress to Impress...

As the days passed, I found myself growing more and more obsessed with impressing Pari. I had a deep connection with her, yet I couldn't muster the courage to confess my feelings. I was just a small boy, unsure of what love really meant, but the emotions I was experiencing were real. This was my version of love, pure and innocent, untouched by the complexities of relationships that adults often talk about.

The world around me was changing, though. In the age of the internet, love had become more accessible, but also more complicated. Foreign movies and series had become a trend, shaping the way young people viewed love. Back then, in my small town, love was still a simple, almost naive concept. You liked someone, and it was pure, without the distractions of modern-day dating culture. There were no multiple crushes, no complicated texting games. You liked someone, and you did everything in your power to show them you cared.

In my case, I was trying to find a way to impress Pari. Sitting next to her made it easier to talk to her, but I still couldn't bring myself to say the words I wanted to. Every time I looked into her eyes, I felt like I would forget every word I had planned to say. Her eyes were like a mirror reflecting the best version of myself, and I couldn't help but get lost in them. It wasn't just the way she looked; it was the way she made me feel. Her smile, her kindness, everything about her seemed perfect, like something out of a dream.

They say "Love is when you sit beside someone doing nothing, but you still feel happy and complete." That was how I felt whenever I was near her. I was filled with happiness, yet I remained silent, not knowing how to express the depth of my feelings. But she didn't know. She didn't know that I was madly in love with her.

I had two options now. One, confess my feelings, but that seemed impossible with my overwhelming fear. The other, try to impress her. I knew it was a ridiculous idea, but it was the only one I had. I couldn't confess, but maybe I could make her notice me.

So, I enlisted the help of my best friend, Anni. He was the only one who knew about my feelings, and I needed his advice. After all, he was the one who had always been there for me. But I knew that helping me wouldn't come for free. Anni wasn't the type to give out favors without expecting something in return.

Our plan was simple: I would try to impress Pari by riding my cycle around her street, doing stunts and hoping she would notice me. It was a silly idea, but I was desperate. I wasn't perfect at stunts, but I could do a few tricks, like wheelies and skids. The idea was to impress her, not make a fool of myself.

The first day of the plan didn't go as I had hoped. I was late, and by the time I reached her street, she was already inside her house. But I kept riding around, hoping to catch a glimpse of her. It felt like a waste of time, but I couldn't stop myself. The next day, however, luck was on my side. Pari was outside, and as I rode past, she waved at me. I was on cloud nine.

The next time we spoke, Pari casually mentioned that she had seen me riding my cycle the previous evening. I was caught off guard. How had she seen me? Her house was on the first floor, and the street was far below. But it didn't matter. She had noticed me. That was enough.

As the days went by, I continued my cycle stunts, hoping to impress her. Slowly, we began to talk more. We became friends, and I felt like I was getting closer to her. But there was one thing I struggled with: my temper. I had a bad habit of getting angry quickly, and when I did, I would lose control. It wasn't something I was proud of, but it was a part of me I couldn't seem to change.

One day, our Hindi teacher called on me to answer a question in class. I answered correctly, but she still made me sit in the front because she thought I wasn't paying attention. I was frustrated, but I didn't show it. I didn't want to embarrass myself in front of Pari. I had to prove to her that I was more than just the boy who got angry all the time. I was determined to focus, to do my best, and to show her that I was someone worth noticing.

It wasn't easy, but I kept trying. I knew that if I wanted to be with Pari, I had to be patient, to prove myself. And maybe, just maybe, one day, she would see me the way I saw her.

As I sat in class, still shaking from the anger I had felt earlier, I tried my best to hide my emotions from Pari. The incident with the teacher had really set me off, and I couldn't shake the frustration. When I had been forced to sit in the front bench, it felt like an unfair punishment, especially after I had answered the question correctly. I knew I shouldn't have let it bother me so much, but I couldn't help it.

After the class, I quickly grabbed a pencil from my desk and snapped it in half, stuffing the pieces into my bag. I was trying to suppress my anger, but it was hard. Pari, however, noticed. She was quiet at first, but then she came over to me during lunch break, her voice soft and comforting.

"Are you alright?" she asked.

I nodded, still not fully able to express what I was feeling.

"You were angry, right? It's okay to be angry, but don't lose your patience," she continued. "I saw you break the pencil and put it in your bag. Maybe, every time you get scolded, you can break a pencil and let out your frustration. It'll help you calm down."

Her words were simple, but they hit me in a way I hadn't expected. She wasn't just being kind; she was trying to help me understand my emotions better. I felt a warmth in my chest, a feeling that only grew as we continued to talk.

That moment became a ritual for us. Whenever I got angry, she would calm me down, and after class, we would break a pencil together. I would collect those broken pencils and store them safely in my desk. Pari never knew I kept them as a reminder of those moments. To her, they were just thrown away, but to me, they were precious.

For a week, everything seemed to be going perfectly. But, as is often the case, life had other plans. One day, while Anni and I were playing in the field, a new kid, Sam, came to join us. He had recently moved into the neighbourhood and seemed eager to make new friends. At first, everything was fine. We played, laughed, and enjoyed the day.

But then, out of nowhere, Sam dropped a bombshell.

"I like Pari," he said.

I froze. My heart pounded in my chest, and anger surged through me. I wasn't prepared for this. Sam had been talking to me casually, but now he was revealing something I wasn't ready to hear. I looked at Anni, and he silently signalled for me to stay calm. But it was hard. My emotions were all over the place.

"Are you willing to help me?" Sam asked, his voice uncertain.

I was furious, but I tried to keep my cool. "Let me see," I replied, my voice tight with anger.

Later, Anni and I had a serious discussion. Sam was now a competitor. I couldn't let him get ahead of me. Pari and I had been talking more, and I was getting closer to her. But now, with Sam in the picture, I had to act fast.

The next day, during a conversation with Pari, she asked about my hobbies. I didn't have any, really. I spent most of my free time playing or catching small fish in streams. I had a small aquarium at home, filled with tiny fish, and I also had a well where I kept bigger ones.

When I told Pari about my fish-keeping hobby, she seemed genuinely interested. "Can I see your tank?" she asked.

This was my chance. I couldn't let this opportunity slip by. "Sure, you can come over on Sunday," I said, trying to hide the excitement in my voice.

I rushed home that evening, eager to prepare. My mom, of course, noticed me cleaning the aquarium. "Why are you cleaning it today?" she asked, raising an eyebrow.

I tried to play it cool. "No one is around to play, so I thought I'd clean it up," I replied, hoping she wouldn't question me further.

The next day, Pari confirmed that she would be coming over on Sunday. I had just one day to prepare everything.

Anni and I spent our lunch break discussing how to redecorate the aquarium. I was determined to make it perfect for her visit.

But then, disaster struck. During class, I started feeling sick—at least, that's what I told the teacher. I asked to leave early, and since I lived close to the school, Anni was asked to accompany me home. It was all part of the plan. Anni and I rushed home, and while I pretended to rest, Anni got to work redecorating the aquarium. We added live plants and made sure everything looked perfect.

But there was one more problem: we needed a small turtle. There was a pond near my house, full of baby turtles, and Anni thought it would be a great addition to the tank. But getting to the pond wasn't going to be easy. We had to cross a field where a strict uncle was working, and if he caught us, we'd be in big trouble.

We waited for the right moment, hiding in a bush until the coast was clear. When we finally reached the pond, we had no idea how to catch the turtles. It wasn't going to be easy, but we were determined.

The plan to get a turtle had been a disaster. We thought it would be easy to catch them, but the little creatures were surprisingly fast in the water. After trying for a while, we ended up catching 12 fish and 4 small crawfish instead. But that created a new problem—if my mom saw the fish, she'd know we had broken the rules and gone to the pond. So, we hid the bottle with the fish in the backyard, hoping she wouldn't notice.

We had to wait until evening, when my mom would go to the temple for her pooja. Once she left, we quickly transferred the fish into the aquarium and made sure everything looked normal.

The next day, Saturday, we went to school for our group activity. It was a fun day, but when I got home later, I found that my mom had already noticed the new fish and crawfish in the aquarium. She didn't waste any time asking, "Did you go to catch the fish again?"

I froze. "No, mom," I said, trying to stay calm.

"Then how did these fish get here?" she asked.

"My friend gave them to me," I replied, quickly making up a story. "His aquarium was full, so he gave them to me."

My heart was pounding, but I managed to get away with the lie. At dinner, I casually mentioned that Pari and her mom would be visiting us on Sunday. Since my mom and Pari's mom were friends, she didn't ask too many questions.

The next day, at school, we had a mass PT session, and I was just going through the motions, trying not to let my mind wander. But then, a fellow student collapsed due to the heat. As usual, I was the one to help him up and carry him to the classroom. Afterward, Pari and I exchanged a few words, but the teacher came in, and we had to keep quiet.

Later that day, we had solo performances, and I was excited to see Pari perform. She was going to dance, and I was determined to be there to watch her. Anni and I made our way to the auditorium, where we had to sit through some very boring performances before Pari finally took the stage.

When she began dancing, I was completely mesmerized. She moved with such grace, like a peacock dancing in the rain. It was as if the whole world around her had slowed down. I felt like I was in a dream, and the way she danced made everything seem magical. When the performance ended, everyone clapped, but I noticed Sam in the front row, whistling. The sight of him made my blood boil.

I was so angry that I couldn't even look at Pari. She called out to me, but I ignored her, too upset to respond. I stormed out of the auditorium, with Anni following me. We went to the boys' washroom, trying to come up with a plan to get Sam out of the way.

But we didn't need to worry for long. The school announced that next Saturday would be an inter-class sports competition, and the teams would be divided by drawing chits. Anni and I were in the same team, the Lions, while Sam ended up in the Tigers team. This was our chance to prove ourselves. If we won, Pari would be impressed, and Sam would be silenced for a while.

The only problem was that we didn't know what sport we'd be playing. The volunteers were supposed to pick between cricket, football, and volleyball. I knew that football was the likely choice, since two of the volunteers were huge football fans. So, I went to one of them, a close friend, and convinced him to pick cricket instead. But I still needed to get the other volunteers on board.

Anni had an idea. One of the volunteers had a crush on a girl in our class, so Anni went up to him and said, "Bro, you should pick cricket. It's her favourite game."

I wasn't sure if that would work, but I decided to take another route. I went to the headmistress and told her that football was too risky and that volleyball would have too many players, making it hard for everyone to perform. I hoped that would sway her decision. We just had to win the game, and I was determined to do whatever it took to impress Pari and show Sam that I was the better choice for her.

I never expected my suggestion to the headmistress to be taken seriously. But when she announced that football could lead to injuries, and that the students could either play cricket or volleyball, I was shocked. If we chose volleyball, substitutions would be mandatory, and everyone would have to play as a team. To my surprise, she took my suggestion, not entirely, but in part.

I knew that once the choice was between cricket and volleyball, everyone would vote for cricket. After all, we had been playing volleyball every day at school, but cricket had always been off-limits. So, as expected, the vote was unanimous, and the school announced that next Saturday, the sports event would be cricket.

I was thrilled. I wasn't the best cricket player, but I was good enough, and Sam—who was my main rival—wasn't as skilled. However, his teammates were strong, and defeating them wouldn't be easy. But I was determined to give it my all.

Amid all the excitement about the sports event, I completely forgot that Pari was visiting my house the next day. The school bell rang, signalling the end of the day, and everyone rushed out. As I was picking up my bag, Pari approached me and casually mentioned, "I'll come over around 4 o'clock tomorrow." That's when it hit me—Pari was coming to see me.

I rushed home that afternoon, quickly finished my lunch, and dove into my homework. I knew that if I didn't finish it today, I wouldn't have time to spend with her tomorrow. My mom, seeing me studying on a Saturday afternoon at 3 o'clock, was utterly shocked. She even took a photo of me—something I still couldn't quite understand. It was the first time I'd ever studied on a Saturday, especially in the afternoon.

"What on earth are you doing?" she asked, clearly baffled.

"I'm doing my homework," I replied.

"Why?" she asked, her tone filled with disbelief.

"Because I have to practice for the match tomorrow, and my friends are visiting in the evening," I explained.

"I think God heard my prayers and changed you," she replied sarcastically.

But I didn't let her comments distract me. I focused on my homework, determined to finish it. I sat for three hours straight, rushing through the work. By 6:20, I had completed everything, though not neatly. But it didn't matter; my homework was done.

The excitement of Pari visiting kept me on edge. I was eager to impress her, but I also had to practice for the match. I gathered the whole team and asked them to join me for a practice session on Sunday at our playground. Little did they know, I was also hoping to impress Pari with my dedication to cricket. They probably thought we were just practicing to win the match.

Sunday arrived, and I woke up at 6 a.m., full of excitement and determination. I couldn't sleep any longer, so I just lay in bed until 8 a.m. After freshening up and having breakfast, I called Anni at 9:45 to make sure everyone would meet at the ground at 10.

When we arrived at the playground at 10 sharp, only two players had shown up. We waited for another 30 minutes, and by the time everyone trickled in, only six of us were present. The rest of the team was nowhere to be seen. We decided to play anyway, but with only six players, we had to make do. We couldn't form two teams of five, so we played single batting. We took the bat, placed it on the ground, and wrote numbers on it, covering the numbers with the bat. Everyone picked a slot, and I ended up with the third number, while Anni got the first.

We began the game, and it was a mix of good and bad plays. Some players were good, but others were terrible at catching the ball and batting. As the game went on, it became clear that our team was unbalanced. We had five solid players, and the rest were either mediocre or downright bad. But we had to make it work if we were going to win the match. The situation felt impossible, but we pushed through, playing until 2 p.m. When we decided to call it a day, one player insisted we keep practicing in the evening. But I couldn't afford to—Pari was coming over, and I had to prepare.

Anni and I headed home, discussing the match and, of course, Pari's visit. Anni congratulated me, though I had no idea why. I guess he assumed I was excited because Pari was coming to my house. I arrived home around 2:15, starving, so I had lunch first before heading straight to the bathroom. My mom had noticed my change in behaviour over the past few days, but she didn't ask any questions.

After freshening up, I started picking out my best outfit. I rummaged through my clothes, scattering them across the room, before finally settling on something I thought would impress Pari. I started cleaning my room, but as I did, I got distracted by a shooting game on my computer. It was one of the most popular games at the time, where you had to aim a gun controller at the screen and shoot birds. I played for an hour, but as the clock ticked closer to 4 p.m., I started to feel nervous. My heart raced as I realized that Pari would be arriving soon.

At 4:07, I checked the clock again. Still no sign of her. Time seemed to slow down, and I anxiously glanced at the clock every minute. Finally, at 4:25, I saw Pari and her mom parking their car at the gate. My heart did a little dance, but I kept my composure. I didn't rush to the door. Instead, I sat on the sofa and pretended to watch TV, letting my mom answer the door.

When they walked in, I finally saw Pari clearly. She was wearing an olive-green top and black jeans, her hair flowing freely in the breeze from the fan. A gust of wind blew through her hair, and she tucked it behind her ear with a graceful motion. She greeted me with a radiant smile, and I couldn't help but stare at her. Her large, dark eyes were framed by kajal, and the small dot of a black bindi on her forehead made her look even more beautiful. I was completely lost in the moment, and all I could do was smile and wave at her.

My mom greeted Pari and her mom, and they began chatting while Pari and I went outside to play. I was so happy that she was at my house, but I was also incredibly nervous. I didn't know what to do next. Eventually, we went to my room, and she asked, "Where's your aquarium?"

I had completely forgotten that she came to see my aquarium. "It's inside. Come, I'll show you," I said, leading her to the room. She was so excited when she saw the aquarium, full of fish swimming gracefully. I proudly told her all about the fish, especially the crawfish, embellishing the story of how I caught them. We spent about ten minutes watching the fish and talking about our shared love of dogs. I told her all about my obsession with German Shepherds.

Soon, my mom called us for coffee, and we went to the hall to enjoy some cake and coffee, which I had begged my dad to buy. Everything was going smoothly until the topic of studies came up. Pari, being the excellent student she was, had no complaints about her grades, but I was a bit of a different story. To my surprise, my mom didn't complain about my studies. In fact, she said, "He's getting better. He's been studying more lately. I don't even know why. I think

God heard my prayers."

I couldn't help but whisper to myself, *Pari is the reason behind it.* Both my mom and Pari's mom laughed, and Pari smiled at me. I smiled back, feeling a little embarrassed but happy at the same time.

"But he's still terrible at Hindi," my mom added, ruining the moment. I shot her an angry look, but she just smiled innocently. Pari and her mom laughed again, and I tried to hide my embarrassment.

Later, we went to my computer to play games, but just as I was showing off my skills, the electricity went out. We didn't have an inverter at the time, so Pari suggested we play Snake and Ladder. I wasn't great at dice games, and I had a knack for getting bad rolls. It was like dice and I were enemies. No matter what number I aimed for, I always got the opposite.

We started the game, and I was quickly bitten by snakes, falling back to earlier spots. Pari, on the other hand, was doing well—until she landed on a snake at 99, sending her all the way back to 13. I couldn't help but feel sorry for her, but deep down, I knew I wouldn't win. I wanted her to win, to be happy.

Despite my bad luck with the dice, I was content. Spending time with Pari, even in the simplest moments, made me feel like the luckiest person in the world.

Love, in its purest form, is made up of the smallest things—the little gestures, the quiet sacrifices, the willingness to lose for someone you care about. Sometimes, it's not about winning at all. It's about seeing the happiness on your partner's face and realizing that their joy makes everything worth it. The feeling of contentment when you see them smile, even if you've lost a game, is beyond comparison. It's a strange kind of happiness—one that fills your heart even in the midst of loss. For me, love isn't a grand, unattainable thing. It's the small, seemingly insignificant moments that come together to create something beautiful.

That day, as we played Snake and Ladder, I knew I was losing. I could feel the dice slipping through my fingers, and I could see the game slipping away from me. But it didn't matter. Pari was laughing, teasing me for my bad luck, and I couldn't help but smile. She had won, and I was happy—not because I had lost, but because she was happy. That's what mattered. Her laughter, her joy, made me forget all about my defeat. It was a strange feeling, but it was exactly what I wanted. To see her smile, to hear her laugh—it was more than enough to make me forget the game.

As the afternoon went on, time seemed to slip away faster than I wanted. Pari's mom called her, saying it was time to go home. That was the moment I had been dreading, the moment I had hoped would never come. The thought of her leaving my house, even though I knew I'd see her again tomorrow at school, brought an unexpected ache to my heart. It wasn't just the end of the visit; it was the feeling of something slipping away, something precious.

Pari and I walked back to the hall, where my mom was offering haladi and kunkum to Pari's mom as a sign of respect. My mom also put kunkum on Pari's forehead, and I couldn't help but smile to myself. I found myself silently wishing that she would take the haladi as well, that maybe one day, she would be my daughter-in-law. It was a fleeting thought, but it made my heart race in a way I hadn't expected.

After a few more minutes of conversation, it was time for Pari and her mom to leave. As they walked toward the door, I stood there, watching them, feeling an odd tightness in my chest. With every step they took away from my house, the pain in my heart grew. I knew I'd see her tomorrow, but in that moment, it felt like I was losing something I didn't want to let go of.

When they reached the scooter, Pari turned around and waved goodbye. That simple wave sent a rush of emotions through me—happiness, longing, and a strange sense of satisfaction all at once. She was leaving, but the memory of her visit, of her smile, would stay with me. I waved back, trying to act normal, though inside, I was a whirlwind of emotions.

As they drove away, I stood there for a few moments longer, watching them disappear down the road. The more distance they put between us, the more it felt like my heart was being tugged. It wasn't just the goodbye—it was the realization that this moment, this day, had been perfect. And now it was over.

That night, I didn't feel like eating dinner. I wasn't hungry, not in the way I usually was. It wasn't sadness exactly, but something close to it. A quiet emptiness lingered in my chest, but it wasn't a painful emptiness—it was more like a calm, peaceful ache. The kind of feeling you get when you know something important has happened, something that will stay with you. I had wanted Pari to come over, and she had. I had wanted her to see my aquarium, and she had. I had wanted to impress her, to make her smile—and I had done that.

As I lay in bed that night, I thought about everything that had happened. I thought about how we had laughed together, how we had talked about dogs and fish, how she had teased me during the game, and how my mom had joked about me studying more. It had all been so simple, yet so perfect.

And even though she was gone, even though the day was over, I knew that our bond had grown stronger. That quiet, unspoken connection between us had deepened. I felt a sense of satisfaction, a quiet happiness that filled my heart. It was a strange, bittersweet feeling, but it was one I wouldn't trade for anything.

I closed my eyes, letting the events of the day replay in my mind. Tomorrow would come, and I would see Pari at school, but for now, I let the memory of her smile, of her visit, stay with me. It was enough. It would always be enough.

3

Tournament...

The next day, when I walked into school, I could feel the usual Monday frustration in the air. Everyone was dreading the start of the week, but I couldn't help but feel excited. Today, I'd see Pari again, and I was eager to talk about everything that had happened yesterday. I arrived early, hoping to catch her before the day got too busy. But as soon as I stepped into class, I remembered something I had completely forgotten about—the morning cricket practice.

I had been so focused on seeing Pari that I hadn't thought about the fact that we had been practicing every morning for Saturday's tournament. I had even convinced everyone to come in early for practice. I couldn't believe I had motivated my classmates to show up. It was both surprising and a little overwhelming. But now, there was no time to chat or relax. I had to go straight to practice.

I didn't even have breakfast that morning, all because I wanted to get to school early. My stomach was growling, and I felt drained. After 30 minutes of intense cricket practice, I was exhausted. As the school bell rang and we headed to the prayer assembly, I felt lightheaded, but I stood tall, not wanting to show any sign of weakness in front of

Pari. I didn't want her to see me in a vulnerable state.

During the assembly, I felt dizzy, but I fought through it. Afterward, I rushed back to the classroom, grabbed some water, and tried to steady myself. I was doing my best to keep it together when Pari noticed me.

"Is everything all right?" she asked, concern in her eyes.

"Yeah, I'm fine," I replied, trying to sound casual, even though I was far from it. I sat down on the bench to rest for a moment, hoping the dizziness would pass.

During the break, I ate some biscuits and drank a lot of water. Slowly, I started to feel better, but my mind kept drifting back to Pari. I was looking forward to spending time with her, but I still had to push through the day.

Our third period was computer class, and it was always a mad rush to grab a computer. There were only 30 computers in the lab, and only 24 of them were in working condition. The latecomers were always left with the worst computers, so I rushed to get a good seat. I made it to a decent spot, but then I noticed Pari was late. She was looking around for a computer, so I waved her over.

"Are you sure?" she asked, eyeing my seat.

I smiled, "Yeah, of course."

I had a computer at home, so it didn't matter to me. I gave her my seat and sat beside her. The others were scrambling for computers, but I was content. For the first time today, I could focus on something other than my exhaustion.

We started talking about yesterday, and she complimented me on my aquarium, asking questions about the fish and the dog breeds I loved. I was so happy that she was genuinely interested in what I had to say. The conversation flowed easily, and for a moment, everything felt perfect.

After class, we had Hindi, but our teacher was absent, so we got a free period. In the afternoon, we had social studies, and then P.T. class. We all decided to ask our social studies teacher to take the class early so we could have more time to play. She was super cool and agreed, leaving us with a full afternoon for cricket practice.

The sun was blazing that day, and the girls stood in the shade, watching us play. Some of them went back to the class, but the boys were playing with all their energy. Everyone was trying their best, especially since the girls were watching. Anni and I were the only ones not playing hard. Anni wasn't interested in impressing anyone—he was always focused on the game. But for me, it was different. I didn't want to play too hard because Pari wasn't out there with us. She had stayed in the class to avoid the sun.

The others started making fun of Anni and me for not playing hard enough. That's when Sam came over and said, "The ball won't hurt if you hit it hard."

Anni, always quick to react, turned to me, his face flushed with anger. "Bro, that dude is making fun of us. We should teach him a lesson."

"Who?" I asked, not fully understanding what was going on.

"Sam," Anni replied, his tone sharp.

I shrugged. "Leave it, dude. It's too hot. We'll show him in the real match."

But Anni wasn't backing down. He was determined to take revenge on Sam. I wasn't too bothered, but Anni knew how to push my buttons. He knew I didn't like being mocked, especially not in front of Pari.

After the match, Anni went inside to get some water, and Sam followed him. Anni had a plan. I didn't know it yet, but I would soon find out. When Anni came back, he called me over in his usual angry tone, using my full name. That was a sign that he was serious.

"Sam was talking to Pari when I went inside to get water," Anni said, his voice low. "He said you and I suck at cricket and laughed."

I was furious. I didn't want to believe it, but I could feel my anger rising. I knew I had to do something. "We'll show them how to play," Anni said, his eyes burning with determination. "We'll show them how to hit a ball."

I agreed. I was ready to take my frustration out on Sam.

The match began, and this time, I decided to bowl first. Sam was on the non-strike side, and I had a plan. I would give him one run to get him on strike, then I would show him what we were made of. But things didn't go as planned. The first ball I bowled was too slow, and Sam hit it for a boundary. Anni was furious with me, but I didn't know how the ball had gone so far.

I tried again, putting more force into the next ball. This time, Sam didn't even touch it. I felt a little better, but I still had one more chance to get him out. The next ball I bowled was a medium-speed delivery, and Sam took a single, bringing him to the strike. Now, my plan was in motion.

I had only three balls left to make Sam regret his words. I bowled the next one with all the power I could muster, but it was a wide ball. Sam looked at me and laughed, a smug smile on his face. It only made me more determined. I was going to make him pay for underestimating us.

The game was really on now. My frustration had reached its peak, and I could feel the adrenaline coursing through me. I grabbed the ball and rubbed my hands in the soil, partly for grip, but mostly for dramatic effect. It was something I had seen in the movies when the hero would rub his hands in the dirt or apply a tilak of soil to his forehead before going into battle. It was as if that small action would unlock some hidden power, a strength that would help him defeat the villain. I don't know why, but in that moment, I felt like I needed that same heroic energy.

I took a deep breath and bowled the ball with all my focus. And it worked. Sam was bowled out. The entire team erupted in cheers, and I couldn't help but let out a grin. I pointed at Sam, signalling that he should head home. The boys were impressed by my delivery, and Anni, ever the supportive friend, came running to me, pulling me into a hug and jumping around in excitement. He even flashed a few fingers at Sam, as if to say, "Take that."

Our classroom was right near the ground, so the sound of the cheering reached Pari. She stepped outside to see what was going on, asking her friend what had happened. I'm sure her friend explained everything to her, and before long, Pari was watching the game. Now, with her eyes on me, I felt the pressure. I had only two balls left to bowl, and I had to make them count.

I rubbed my hands in the soil once again, trying to channel that same energy. The next ball I bowled was high, just missing the wicket by an inch. The crowd groaned, and I felt a pang of frustration. I had hoped to impress Pari, but now I was doubting myself. "Don't worry," I told myself. "One more ball."

But when the batsman hit the next ball and ran a single, I felt like I had missed my chance. I had hoped to make an impact, to show Pari what I was capable of, but now I had failed. I felt like a failure.

Anni, sensing my frustration, came up to me with a grin. "The last two balls you bowled had more effort than the first four, I know why," he said, his eyes twinkling.

"Yeah, but I had a chance to impress her and I ruined it," I muttered, still feeling down.

Anni, ever the optimist, patted me on the back. "Don't worry, you play strike first. I'll take the non-strike," he said, a smile on his face.

I was touched by his support. Anni was always the one who took the strike in our matches, but he was offering it to me now. It meant a lot. I had been so focused on impressing Pari that I had forgotten what really mattered—the game, my teammates, and the support we gave each other.

After we finished bowling, the score was 45/4 in 6 overs. It was our turn to bat, and I needed to be strategic. I asked Anni to take the strike for the first two balls and then give me the chance to face the bowlers. He agreed without hesitation.

The bowlers were fast and aggressive, but Anni managed to defend the first ball and took a single on the second, passing the strike to me. Now, I was ready. I had watched how they were bowling, and I knew how to respond. The third ball came at me, and I defended it, not wanting to give away my plans just yet.

But when the fourth ball came, I knew exactly what to do. The bowler was overconfident, having seen that we had only scored one run from the first three balls. Our teammates, who weren't as skilled at cricket, started shouting for us to hit the ball and get some runs. I could feel the pressure, but I was determined. I swung the bat with all my might, and the ball flew, just missing the six mark but landing as a boundary.

Anni gave me a thumbs up from the non-strike, and I felt a sense of accomplishment, but I wasn't satisfied. I wanted a six. The bowler, sensing my confidence, bowled the next ball even harder. This time, I swung with all my frustration, and the ball soared into the sky. It was a six.

The crowd erupted in cheers, and I looked over at Pari. She was clapping, smiling at me. That was all I needed to see. I was happy. But there was still one ball left, and I knew I had to make it count.

The bowler sent the final ball toward me, but it turned unexpectedly as it approached. I knew I couldn't hit it for a six, but I could still get two runs. I had to be strategic, though. If I didn't make it, I would be back on strike, and Anni wouldn't get his turn. So, I defended the ball and signalled to Anni not to run.

Anni, confused, came up to me after the over. "Why did you tell me not to run?" he asked.

"You also need to play, right?" I replied, my voice steady.

Anni smiled, understanding. We came to an agreement: he would play the first three balls, and I would play the next three. Anni took the strike, and he scored two boundaries. On the third ball, he gave me the strike, and we were feeling confident.

But as I stepped up to bat, I got a little overconfident. On the fourth ball, I tried to hit the ball for another six, aiming for the spot where Pari was standing. The ball flew toward her, and I watched in disbelief as she caught it and threw it to the ground.

The next ball came, and I tried to hit it to her side again, but this time the ball hit the edge of my bat and went high. The keeper caught it, and I was out.

Anni was shocked, and I could see the disappointment in his eyes. But even though I had been out at a crucial moment, I knew our team was still in a strong position. We had scored 26/1 in the second over, and there were still 4 more overs to go. We only needed 20 more runs to win, and I had complete faith in our teammates.

Even when Anni got out at 41/2 in the fourth over, I knew we had it in the bag. Our teammates, despite their lack of experience, played with every ounce of stamina they had. They scored the remaining 5 runs in just 5 balls, and we won the match. It wasn't the perfect game for me, but it was a victory, and that was what mattered.

That week was a blur of practice and games. I had been so focused on the tournament that I hadn't realized I was playing to impress Pari. I had stopped talking to her, not because I didn't want to, but because I had been consumed by the match.

Friday came, the last day of our practice. Anni and I were heading home when we stopped at our regular shop to grab some juice. As we were leaving, we saw Pari and her dad. I thought about talking to her, but her dad was a teacher, and I had always been intimidated by teachers, especially those who weren't in our school. I decided against it, feeling a bit nervous.

Later that evening, when I was searching for my sports pants at home, I found something unexpected. A small piece of pearl caught my eye. I picked it up, and my heart skipped a beat. It was Pari's earring. I remembered that it had a pearl in it, and I realized it must have fallen off when she was at my house. Holding that pearl in my hand, I felt a rush of happiness. It felt like an antique piece, something precious.

I wrapped it carefully in a piece of paper and placed it in an envelope. Then, I stored it in a file with my other important documents, including my mark sheets. It felt like a secret treasure, something that connected me to her in a way I couldn't explain.

The next day was the tournament, and I received a reward for the match we had played the day before. But in my heart, I knew that the real victory wasn't the match—it was the small moments, the connections, and the memories that I would carry with me forever

It was a Saturday morning, and I woke up at 6 AM, the excitement of the match already buzzing in my veins. I needed to get warmed up, so I joined my dad for a jog. The cool morning air hit my face, helping me clear my mind and focus. We ran through the quiet streets, the rhythmic sound of our footsteps grounding me. By 7 AM, we were back home. I took a quick shower, got dressed, and had a light breakfast. My stomach churned with anticipation for the match ahead.

As I entered the school, I saw Pari already sitting at her bench in the classroom. I walked to my seat, and when I glanced at her, she smiled at me. My heart skipped a beat.

"Are you ready for the match today?" she asked, her voice light and friendly.

"Yes, I'm excited," I replied, trying to sound calm, though my mind was racing.

"I saw you playing yesterday. You play well," she said, and I felt a rush of warmth.

"No, I play, but I can't play well," I replied, my voice almost a whisper. But in my head, I was thinking, *if you hadn't been there to watch, I probably wouldn't have even played.*

As we continued talking about yesterday's match, Pari suddenly looked at me and said, "You have a nice smile."

The words hit me like a bolt of lightning. My cheeks flushed, and I could feel the heat spreading across my face. I quickly looked down, too shy to look her in the eye. Imagine your crush telling you that you're beautiful—that's exactly how I felt in that moment.

She smiled again and said, "Don't be shy."

"I'm not shy," I stammered, but I could feel my face betraying me.

"I can see," she teased, and I couldn't help but laugh nervously.

Before I could say anything else, the school bell rang, signalling the start of assembly. We all lined up and headed to the ground for the morning prayer. As usual, there was the guy in front of me who fainted right after the national anthem. I had to help him back to the classroom, give him some glucose and water, and make sure he was okay before going back to the PT session. By the time I arrived, it was already halfway over.

After PT, we went back to class for attendance. The match was about to begin, and the nerves started to settle in. We went to the locker room to change into our gear. As I was putting on my shoes, I suddenly felt a sharp cramp in my knee. I didn't know where it came from. I hadn't fallen or twisted it, but the pain was real. It felt like a sprain, and I was worried it would affect my performance.

I called over Anni. "Can you help me out? Pull my leg and see if you can fix it."

Anni gave my leg a firm tug, and there was a loud popping sound, like a knuckle cracking. The pain eased immediately, and I felt better.

We warmed up with some light jumping and stretching, then headed straight to the ground. As we were in the higher primary group, our match was the first one of the days. We walked up to the pitch for the toss, and to our relief, we won.

Our teammates immediately asked me to take the bat, but I knew that if we batted first and set a target, they would have a good chance of chasing it down. If we bowled first, we would know exactly how many runs we needed to defend. It was a strategic decision, and though the team wasn't thrilled about it, I was confident it was the right call.

"We'll bowl first," I said, my voice firm. "Trust me, it's the best option for us."

Anni was the first to bowl. Our plan was that Sam, who was standing on the non-strike, would eventually come to the strike, and that's when I would bowl to him. It would be my chance to impress Pari, and teach Sam a lesson for laughing at me. He had a crush on her too, so it felt like a perfect opportunity to show him who was really in control. It was like hitting three birds with one stone—impressing Pari, proving myself, and putting Sam in his place.

But to our surprise, Sam was already standing on the strike side as Anni prepared to bowl. He looked at me and, without a word, passed the ball to me. I exchanged a quick glance with Anni, who smiled knowingly. I took a deep breath, trying to calm my nerves, and walked up to the pitch, ready to bowl.

Just as I was running to bowl the first ball, the cramp in my leg came back. It shot through my knee, making every step feel like a battle. But I pushed through the pain, determined not to let it stop me. I bowled the first ball, and Sam hit it, but it didn't go far. One of our fielders caught it, and we had our first wicket. I felt a brief sense of relief, but I still wasn't satisfied.

I bowled the next ball with everything I had, and it went fast. Sam defended it again, but I could feel the weight of the pain in my leg. I couldn't get into my rhythm, and I struggled to generate the power I needed. Despite the discomfort, I pushed on, determined to make the most of the over. By the end of it, I hadn't given away a single run, and I had taken one wicket—but it wasn't Sam's. That was the wicket I wanted, and I felt a twinge of disappointment.

Then, as I was walking back to my teammates, I remembered something. The guy who had fainted earlier in assembly was on our team, and we were one player short. I quickly approached the PT teacher and asked if one player could bowl two overs. After a brief discussion, the teacher agreed, and I was allowed to bowl again.

I walked back to the pitch, my resolve stronger than ever. I knew I had to give everything I had for the team. And for Pari. This match wasn't just about cricket; it was about proving myself, showing what I was capable of, and maybe, just maybe, winning her attention.

After getting another chance to bowl, I called Anni over. "When Sam comes to strike, don't take his wicket. Just bowl to him, but don't let him get out," I said. Anni nodded, understanding the plan.

Anni bowled his over, giving away just 3 runs. Now, it was my turn again, the third over of the match. This was my second—and last—chance to take revenge on Sam. I knew I had to make it count. I took a deep breath, focusing all my energy on the ball. As I ran up to bowl, I threw the ball with everything I had. It was so fast that Sam didn't even have time to react. The ball zipped past him, and our wicketkeeper tried to catch it, but it was traveling too fast. He missed and injured his hand in the process. The speed of that ball was something I had never felt before.

I didn't let up. The next ball, I threw with the same intensity, and this time, the ball hit the stumps. Sam was out. I felt a surge of triumph, but when I looked up, I saw Pari clapping for me. She was supporting our team, and that moment filled me with pride. Maybe, just maybe, I had finally impressed her.

Anni ran over to me, and we shared a celebratory dab. Sam, on the other hand, was fuming. He was angry, not just because he got out, but because I had bowled so fiercely. His pride was wounded, and I could see the frustration in his eyes.

The match continued, and their team managed only 47 runs in 10 overs. It was now our turn to bat. I knew Sam would be bowling against me, and I was ready for it. I turned to Anni and said, "You take the strike. I'll play non-strike. Give me Sam's over. I'll handle him."

Anni agreed, and we got to work. In the first over, Anni single-handedly scored 10 runs. Then, it was my turn. I walked to the crease, knowing Sam was coming for me. There was a silent tension between us. He wanted revenge, and I was ready to face him head-on.

The first ball came in fast, and I tried to defend it, but the ball missed my bat and hit my knee—the same knee that had been cramping earlier. Pain shot through me, and I couldn't help but scream. It was excruciating. But I didn't want Sam to see my weakness. I controlled the pain, forcing myself to focus. Anni asked if I was okay, but I just nodded, signalling that I was fine.

The next ball came in, and this time, I wasn't going to let it pass. I swung with all my might, and the ball flew to the boundary. I stared at Sam as he watched me, his expression a mix of anger and disbelief. The next ball came, and I hit it for a six. The crowd cheered, and I could feel the adrenaline pumping through my veins. I wasn't going to let Sam get the better of me.

I didn't stop there. The next ball went for another boundary. By the end of the second over, we had scored 28 runs. In the following overs, Anni added 10 runs, and I added 12 more. We had reached our target in just 4 overs. We won the match, and as I looked up, I saw Pari clapping and jumping with joy. The victory was sweet, but seeing

Pari so happy made it even sweeter.

After the match, Pari came over to me. "You played really well," she said, her smile wide and genuine.

"Thank you," I replied, feeling my heart race.

We sat together, watching the other teams play. Anni came over to talk to me, but I waved him off. He smiled and whispered, "Enjoy," before walking away. I was content. The day had been perfect.

We spent the rest of the afternoon watching the matches and talking. It was one of the best days of school I had ever had. From that day on, I felt more confident around Pari. We became close friends. She started sharing all the gossip she knew, and we spent a lot of time together. She even started sharing her lunch with me, and I couldn't help but feel a sense of happiness every time we sat together.

Days passed, and everything seemed perfect. But then, one day, I decided I needed to confess my feelings to her. I had been thinking about it for a while, but the fear of rejection kept me from saying anything. I tried to gather the courage, but when I went to talk to her, I overheard her conversation with a friend. They were talking about relationships, and Pari said, "I'm not interested in relationships right now."

My heart sank. I froze, unsure of what to do. If I confessed now, I feared I might lose her as a friend too. I walked away, my mind a whirlwind of doubt and confusion.

Two days later, we were talking again, and I decided to ask her about relationships. I wasn't ready to confess, but I wanted to understand her perspective. "What do you think about relationships?" I asked casually.

She looked at me, confused. "Why?"

"No reason," I replied, trying to keep my tone light.

She smiled and said, "Aren't we too young to be in a relationship?"

"Yeah, you're right," I said, trying to hide my disappointment.

We both fell silent for a moment. I wanted to ask more, but I was too scared to push it further. The conversation ended, and I walked away, feeling like I had missed my chance.

But then, something strange happened. Every time I passed by her, she would look at me and smile. I didn't know what it meant, but it felt like a sign. Was she giving me a hint? I wasn't sure, but I couldn't help but feel a flicker of hope.

Our conversations became more frequent, and we spent more time together. It was like nothing had changed, and yet everything had. I was happier than I had ever been, and the bond between us grew stronger each day. I still didn't know if she felt the same way, but I couldn't help but cherish every moment we spent together. For now, I was content with being close to her, enjoying the moments we shared, and hoping that maybe, someday, she would feel the same way.

As the final exams approached, the atmosphere at school changed. Everyone became more serious, focused on their studies. Groups were formed to study, and it seemed like everyone had a purpose. I, being an average student, found myself in the group of students who needed help. Pari, on the other hand, was an exceptionally intelligent student, and she was often the one helping others. But unfortunately, I was left to study alone in the subjects I struggled with—Hindi and Maths.

For the other subjects, I managed to keep up, and I ended up helping some of my classmates with their studies.

Despite this, I couldn't shake the feeling that a gap had formed between me and Pari. We had been so close before, but now, with exams taking up all our time, we barely spoke. I understood, though. This was a difficult time for everyone, and there was no rush to confess anything. We were both focused on our exams. I told myself that once the exams were over, things would go back to normal.

Pari started to smile at me whenever I passed by, and I couldn't help but feel a flicker of hope. It seemed like maybe she was starting to feel something too, but I didn't want to jump to conclusions. I knew I had to focus on my studies because if I didn't do well in the exams, I wouldn't have any reason to talk to her.

As the days passed, we spent less time together. The exams were the priority, and we only spoke during lunch breaks. Some of our classmates even started teasing us about sitting together during lunch, so we stopped hanging out there too. The focus was entirely on the exams now. For two weeks, I gave up everything else—no distractions, just studying. My parents were impressed by my dedication, and they rewarded me with chocolates. I couldn't help but share them with Pari during the afternoons. It felt good to do something for her, even if it was small.

The exam days arrived, and the schedule was tough. We had 18 days of exams—12 days for the main subjects and 6 days for secondary subjects like arts and crafts. During the main exams, Pari and I were in separate rooms, so we couldn't talk. It felt like a punishment to be so close to her and yet unable to communicate. I tried to talk to her in my mind, wishing for the exams to be over so I could finally speak to her again.

After the main exams, during the arts and crafts days, we all sat together again. These were the last days of school, and the teachers were more lenient with us. The exams would finish by the afternoon, and we had the option to leave or stay at school. I chose to stay, not because I had any particular reason, but because Pari was staying too. I didn't know why she stayed, but I couldn't bring myself to leave when she was there.

Something had changed. It was no longer me starting the conversations. Pari began initiating them. She seemed more comfortable around me, and I couldn't help but feel that maybe she was starting to develop feelings for me. I was overjoyed. It felt like a sign, and I took it as one. I thought maybe this was the moment I had been waiting for.

It was the last day of school, and we were talking as usual. Out of nowhere, Pari asked, "That day, you asked me about my perspective on relationships. What's yours?"

I froze. This was it. The opportunity I had been waiting for. I had a chance to finally tell her how I felt. My heart raced. We had been talking about something completely unrelated—Temple Run, of all things—and now, suddenly, she brought up relationships. It felt like fate.

I knew this was my moment, but for some reason, I couldn't bring myself to say it. The thought of confessing scared me. It was the last day of school, and we had two months of vacation ahead of us. If she rejected me, at least the awkwardness would fade over time. I would only have to see her on results day, and then we could act normal again. But I hesitated, and in that moment of fear, I made a mistake.

I smiled nervously and said, "We're too young for relationships."

The words came out before I could stop them. It was the same answer I had given her before. The moment passed, and I felt like an idiot. I had just ruined my chance.

Pari looked at me, her eyes sparkling with amusement. She smiled and said, "You're repeating what I said."

I laughed awkwardly, but inside, I was beating myself up. I had missed my chance, and now, the moment was gone.

The bell rang, signalling the end of the day. Pari gave me a smile I hadn't seen before. Her eyes were wide, and her pupils dilated as she looked at me. She smiled even more brightly and offered me a handshake. "Bye. I'll see you after the holidays," she said, her voice warm.

In that moment, I realized the truth. I wouldn't see her for months. I wouldn't be able to talk to her or spend time with her like I had during the school year. A wave of sadness washed over me as I watched her walk toward the gate. I rushed to catch up, but by the time I reached the gate, her car had already driven off. I stood there, feeling a lump form in my throat. Tears welled up in my eyes, but I quickly wiped them away. I couldn't let myself break down, not now.

I went home feeling empty. I called Anni, wanting to talk to him about everything that had happened. When he arrived at our regular hangout spot, I told him everything—how I had messed up my chance to confess to Pari, how I had let fear stop me.

Anni listened carefully and then scolded me. "It was the perfect time! Why didn't you tell her?" he asked.

"I know," I replied, feeling the weight of my mistake. "By the time I realized it, it was too late."

Anni shook his head. "Forget it. It's not over yet. Remember, results are on April 11th. That's a Sunday, and it's your birthday!"

"So?" I asked, not understanding at first.

"Idiot," Anni said, grinning. "Your birthday is the perfect opportunity. You'll meet Pari on your birthday. You can tell her how you feel then. It'll be the perfect time!"

The idea hit me like a lightning bolt. I had a chance after all. It would be my birthday, and if she rejected me, it wouldn't be as awkward since it was my special day. I had the advantage, and I couldn't let it slip away.

For the next ten days, Anni and I worked on a plan. We practiced how I would confess, but I had no idea how to express my feelings. So, we turned to old Kannada movies for inspiration. We didn't have much internet access, just 100 MB of data a day, so we watched movies on TV. We spent hours analysing the dialogues, trying to find the perfect words. But we made a mistake—whenever a song came on, we would skip it. We didn't realize that the songs often had the best lines for expressing emotions.

After four days of watching movies, we finally came up with a few lines. But they didn't feel right. They didn't have the impact I was looking for. We still hadn't found the perfect words, but I knew one thing for sure: I had to tell Pari how I felt, no matter what.

After four days of obsessively watching old Kannada movies, trying to find the perfect line to confess my feelings to Pari, Anni and I started to wonder what was going wrong. We had watched countless romantic scenes, analysed dialogues, and even written down the most beautiful lines we could find. But somehow, none of them felt right. None of the lines captured the depth of what I wanted to say.

Frustrated, we decided to change our approach. "Maybe we've been overthinking it," Anni suggested one afternoon, as we sat in our usual spot, surrounded by notebooks and movie scripts. "What if we just focus on the songs instead of the dialogues?"

At first, I was sceptical. How could a song help me express something as complex as my feelings for Pari? But we were running out of time—just two days left until my birthday, and I had to get it right. So, we dove into the world of old songs, the kind that had a timeless quality to them, songs that were filled with raw emotion. As we sifted through lyrics, something clicked. We found line after line that spoke directly to the heart, lines that resonated with the feelings I had for Pari.

That's when I realized something important: the songs were telling me exactly what I needed to hear. Love wasn't about grand gestures or rehearsed speeches; it was about feeling. The lyrics weren't just words—they were an expression of something deeper, something that couldn't be fully captured in any language. Love was an emotion that transcended vocabulary, and the right words didn't always have to be perfect.

But as Anni and I practiced these lines, something else became clear. They felt... forced. The words didn't flow naturally. They seemed rehearsed, almost cringy, as if we were trying too hard to make it sound like a scene from a movie. I could see it in Anni's face too. We both felt the same way. The more we practiced, the less genuine it seemed.

By the eighth day, we were both exhausted and frustrated. "This isn't working," I said, slumping into the chair. "We've been at this for days, and I still don't feel ready."

Anni nodded in agreement. "Maybe we've been looking for the wrong thing. We've been trying to find the perfect words, but maybe what we need is just to speak from the heart."

I sat there, thinking about it. He was right. All this time, I had been so focused on finding the perfect line, the perfect way to express myself. But the truth was, no words could truly capture what I felt for Pari. It wasn't about the speech or the lines—it was about the connection between us, the feelings that had been growing inside me.

So, we decided to scrap the whole plan. We would keep it simple. No more rehearsed lines or borrowed words from movies. I would just speak from the heart. After all, love wasn't something that could be neatly packaged into a sentence. It wasn't about impressing her with my vocabulary—it was about being honest, being real.

"Sometimes, words don't matter," I said, more to myself than to Anni. "What matters is the feeling you have. Words can only go so far. But love... love doesn't need words. It just needs two hearts that understand each other, two people who are right for each other. I'll just tell her how I feel, simply and honestly. That's all that matters."

Anni smiled, clearly relieved. "Exactly. Keep it simple. Tell her how you feel, and let your heart do the talking."

That night, I went to bed with a strange sense of peace. For the first time in days, I wasn't stressing over how to say the right thing. I knew that whatever happened, I had to be true to myself. I had to be brave enough to speak my truth, no matter how simple or imperfect it might be.

The next morning, I woke up with a sense of determination. My birthday was just around the corner, and with it, the chance to finally tell Pari how I felt. I didn't know what the outcome would be, but I knew one thing for sure: I couldn't let fear hold me back any longer.

As the days passed, I kept reminding myself of what mattered most: my feelings for Pari were real, and I didn't need a perfect speech to express them. Love was about connection, not perfection. And when the time came, I would speak from my heart.

4

Moving Apart...

Finally, the day had arrived—the results day. It was a day that should have been filled with excitement and anticipation, but for me, it was different. This was the first and last results day where I felt happy and at peace. Most of my classmates were anxious, dreading the moment they would see their marks, but I was confident. I knew I had worked hard, and even if I didn't get the marks I was hoping for, I was certain I'd do better than last year. And, on top of it all, it was my birthday.

My parents woke me up with cheerful birthday wishes. I got up, freshened up, and went to the temple with them, as was our tradition. Afterward, we came home, and I handed out chocolates to my classmates and teachers, something I always did on my birthday. As I was on my way to school, riding my bicycle, I couldn't shake the feeling of excitement. It wasn't just the results—it was also the thought of seeing Pari again after ten long days.

When I arrived at school, Anni was already there, waiting for me. As soon as I entered the school gates, he greeted me with a grin. "Happy Birthday, dude!" he said, patting me on the back. I thanked him, and he gave me a knowing look. "All the best, man. Don't be afraid this time. Tell her how you feel."

I nodded, feeling a little more confident with his encouragement. We walked to our classroom together, and as we were chatting, the door opened, and Pari entered the room. I was so caught up in our conversation that I didn't notice her at first, but as soon as I saw her, my heart skipped a beat. She smiled at me, and I couldn't help but smile back. Anni, sitting nearby, punched me lightly in the stomach and pointed toward her with a sly grin.

I felt a rush of happiness seeing her again. It had been so long since we'd really talked. Anni, sensing the moment, moved back to his bench, giving me some space. Pari walked over and sat next to me, smiling as she did. "Happy Birthday," she said, her voice as sweet as ever. That simple greeting, coming from her, made my heart flutter. She extended her hand for a handshake, and when I touched it, I felt an electric warmth spread through me. After so many days of not talking, that touch made my birthday feel even more special.

But something was different. I noticed that Pari didn't seem as happy as usual. There was a sadness in her eyes, something I couldn't quite place. It was subtle, but it was there. I didn't know what it was, but I couldn't shake the feeling that something was wrong.

After a while, our teacher arrived and posted the results on the board. The entire class rushed to see their marks, and Pari and I joined the crowd. At first, I didn't check my own marks. I was more concerned with hers. I could sense her unease, and I wanted to know how she had done. When I saw her marks—97%—I couldn't help but feel a rush of pride. She was the topper of the class, and I was so happy for her. She deserved it.

But when I finally checked my own marks, I was stunned. I had scored 89.4%, the highest I had ever gotten in the past three years. It was a significant improvement, and I couldn't stop smiling. I was proud of myself, but there was still something nagging at the back of my mind. I needed to find Pari.

I searched the classroom, but she wasn't there. So, I decided to go to the staff room to distribute chocolates to the teachers. As I entered, every teacher wished me a happy birthday. When I approached my Hindi teacher, she smiled at me and said, "You've really improved this year. Well done."

"Thank you, ma'am," I replied, feeling a little embarrassed but proud at the same time. I continued my way to the office to give chocolates to the clerks, but as I entered the office, I overheard a conversation that would change everything.

One of the office clerks was speaking to another, asking them to prepare a transfer certificate for Pari. My heart stopped. I wasn't sure if I had heard it right, but the words struck me like a bolt of lightning. Pari was leaving? I ran out of the office, unable to process what I had just heard. My heart was racing, and I couldn't breathe. The thought of losing her, especially on my birthday, felt like the cruellest joke.

I stood there, frozen, trying to make sense of it all. And then, I heard her voice—Pari's voice. It had always filled me with warmth and joy, but this time, it was different. It felt distant, like a soft echo of the happiness it used to bring me. I didn't want to hear it. I didn't want to know that she was leaving. I gathered all my courage and turned to face her.

"I'm moving to a new city," Pari said softly. "I'll be changing schools. I'm leaving this town for Bengaluru."

The words hit me like a punch to the gut. I couldn't breathe. The pain was unbearable. It wasn't just the fact that she was leaving—it was the realization that I had never told her how I felt. The words I had kept inside for so long now felt like a weight, pressing down on my chest. I had missed my chance, and now she was slipping away from me.

"Oh, yeah. I heard someone talking about it," I said, trying to sound casual, but my voice cracked.

Pari looked at me, her expression soft. "I wanted to tell you myself, but my mom must have told someone in the staff room."

I nodded, not knowing what to say. "Where are you moving to?" I asked, though I already knew the answer.

"Bengaluru," she replied.

I shook my head, unable to process what was happening. My mind was racing, but my heart was heavy with regret. I had let this moment slip away, and now it was too late.

I couldn't help but notice that she seemed sad too. Was it because of the move? Or was it because of me? I didn't know. All I knew was that I felt like a fool. If I had confessed my feelings to her when I had the chance, maybe things would have turned out differently. But now, all I had were regrets.

The pain of unspoken words, of feelings left unsaid, was worse than any rejection. The question I had never asked haunted me. I had chosen to love her in silence, thinking that would protect me from rejection. But now, I realized that silence had only caused me more pain.

There's a saying: *Express before it's too late. Love before it's gone. Feel before it ends. Hold before it leaves.* I had chosen to keep my feelings locked away, but now I understood that unsaid feelings hurt more than anything else.

Later that day, there was a program to announce the summer holidays. I was trying to hold myself together, but it was hard. As the program ended, I saw Pari one last time. She waved at me, her car already pulling away. I stood there, watching her leave, my heart breaking with every passing second. I wanted to tell her everything, to let her know how much I cared, but all I could do was watch her disappear from my life.

My eyes refused to watch her leave, but my tears came anyway, blurring my vision. And in that moment, I realized that sometimes, the hardest part of love isn't the rejection—it's the silence. The silence that comes when you never say the words you need to say.

As I pedalled home, the weight of the day's events hung heavily on my shoulders. The joy of my birthday and the excitement of my results were overshadowed by the gnawing pain in my chest. I had hoped that seeing Pari one last time would bring some sense of closure, but instead, it had only deepened the wound. I couldn't escape the truth: she was leaving.

When I arrived home, my mom immediately noticed something was off. She asked if I had failed any subjects, her voice laced with concern. I shook my head and handed her my marks card, hoping she wouldn't see through my facade. As she looked at it, a smile spread across her face. "Very good! You've improved a lot. Keep it up!" she said.

But I couldn't share her excitement. I was numb. I didn't want to admit it, but I felt empty inside. I lied, telling her that some dust had gotten in my eye on the way home, but she didn't buy it. She leaned in and blew gently on my eye, as if trying to soothe my pain.

When my dad arrived, he was just as thrilled about my marks. "Great job! Keep improving like this, and you'll do even better next time," he said, his voice full of pride. He was so happy, in fact, that he insisted on taking me out for lunch to celebrate.

I couldn't say no. I knew how much it meant to him, so I smiled and agreed. "Are you alright?" he asked, his voice tinged with concern. "You don't seem excited today. What happened?"

I shook my head, not wanting to burden him with the truth. "Nothing, Dad. Can I invite Anni to join us for lunch?" I asked.

He agreed without hesitation, and soon Anni's dad was on the phone, inviting him to join us. Anni didn't know the full story. He didn't know about Pari leaving, and he certainly didn't know about my unspoken feelings for her. He probably thought I was throwing a party because she had accepted me.

About thirty minutes later, Anni arrived at my house. I was sitting in my room, trying to distract myself by playing on the computer. I didn't want my parents to see how upset I was, so I kept to myself. Anni entered the room, his face lighting up when he saw me. "What did she say? It's all done, right?" he asked, his voice filled with anticipation.

I swallowed hard. "Pari is leaving town," I said quietly.

"What?!" Anni exclaimed, his eyes wide with disbelief.

"Yeah, it's all finished," I replied, my voice flat.

Anni looked at me for a moment, then shrugged. "Leave it. We'll see what happens."

"There's nothing to see," I muttered.

Just then, my dad entered the room, and the conversation came to an abrupt end. He asked us to get ready for lunch, and we headed out to the car. My dad handed me the keys and asked me to pull the car out of the garage. It was the first time I was driving the car by myself.

For most boys, it would have been the happiest day of their lives, but for me, it was the worst.

I managed to pull the car out, but the weight of the day's emotions made it feel like a burden. I handed the keys back to my dad, and Anni and I climbed into the backseat. Anni kept glancing at me, probably wondering how I was holding up.

We arrived at the restaurant, which my dad co-owned. As soon as we walked in, the employees greeted me with smiles and birthday wishes. I forced a smile in return, but it felt like my face was frozen. We were led to the family cabin, and as we were about to order, I saw a familiar face.

It was Pari. And her family.

My heart sank. The surprise was not the good kind. If it had been any other day, I might have been overjoyed to see her, but today it felt like a cruel twist of fate. My mom noticed them and invited them to join us, and I had no choice but to smile and greet them.

As we sat down to eat, Pari's mom mentioned that they were moving because of her job transfer. My heart shattered. I couldn't even look at Pari properly. The food, which was usually delicious, tasted bland. I was hungry, but I couldn't bring myself to eat.

After lunch, my mom invited Pari and her family to the birthday party. But as luck would have it, they were going to another wedding that evening and politely declined. I was relieved, but at the same time, it felt like the universe was toying with me.

When we got home, the party was already in full swing. Relatives and friends had arrived, and I was expected to put on a happy face. But inside, I was drowning. I was the only one not smiling, the only one not enjoying the celebration.

Anni arrived late, and I immediately sought him out. He was the only one who knew what I was going through. I asked him to stay with me throughout the party, and he did, silently supporting me as I pretended to enjoy the festivities.

At one point, my dad insisted I meet some of his business partners. I reluctantly complied, but I couldn't shake the feeling that I was just going through the motions. I wanted the party to end, but it seemed to drag on forever.

Finally, it was time to cut the cake. I went through the motions, smiling for the camera, pretending to be happy. But when the guests began to leave, I excused myself.

"I'm going to bed. I'm feeling tired," I told my mom, my voice barely above a whisper.

She made me a bed on the couch, and I lay down, but sleep wouldn't come. Every time I closed my eyes, I saw Pari's face. I turned and turned, but the images wouldn't fade. My body was exhausted, but my mind was wide awake, trapped in a cycle of pain and regret.

I didn't realize how much I loved her until that moment, lying in the dark, tears welling up in my eyes. I cried for her, hoping that somehow, in some way, she would be mine.

The next morning, I woke up as if I hadn't slept at all. I got ready and told my mom I was going to Anni's house to play. I couldn't stay home. I didn't want anyone to see how broken I was.

Anni and I went to the ground to play, but I wasn't in the mood. I didn't want to ruin his mood, so I decided to leave. I needed to get away from everything, to clear my head.

I asked my mom if I could go to my grandparents' village for the summer. She agreed, and the next day, my dad dropped me off there. The village was a peaceful place, surrounded by lush forests and coffee plantations. It was a world away from the chaos of my life, and for a while, I was able to find some solace.

I spent my days exploring the village, spending time with my grandpa, and taking care of the animals. The pain of Pari leaving never fully went away, but the quiet of the village helped ease it, if only a little.

As the summer drew to a close, I realized that no matter how far I ran, the pain would always be with me. I was still haunted by the thought of Pari, by the words I never said, the love I never confessed.

When my parents came to pick me up, I felt a sense of relief, but also sadness. I had spent so much time in the village, surrounded by nature, that I had almost forgotten the pain. But now, as I left, it was like stepping back into the reality I had tried to escape.

I went back home, but the pain of losing Pari never truly left. It became a part of me, a scar that would always remind me of the one that got away.

And so, I learned the hardest lesson of all: some stories are meant to remain unfinished, but that doesn't make them any less meaningful. Regret is a heavy burden, but it's a part of life. And sometimes, the only way to heal is to let go and move forward, no matter how much it hurts.

5

Every Mile Matters...

I came back to town with my parents, and while I missed my grandparent's house, there was a sense of relief that I didn't expect. The quiet, open space of the village had given me a temporary escape from the ache in my heart, but now, with just three days left before school reopened, I was dreading the return. I wasn't ready to face the same halls, the same classrooms, the same memories that haunted me.

One afternoon, I had to go to my dad's warehouse on the outskirts of town. To get there, we had to pass by the school, and as I looked at the familiar building, a wave of negative energy washed over me. I didn't know why, but I could feel it deep inside. The school, once a place of learning and friendship, now felt like a prison of memories—memories I wasn't ready to confront. I wanted to burn the whole place down, just to erase the past.

When I reached the warehouse, I sat in my dad's cabin, trying to shake the feeling that had settled in my chest. I couldn't go back there. I couldn't face the same classrooms, the same corridors that had witnessed my first love—a love I never had the courage to confess. The thought of seeing her again, knowing she would be gone forever, felt unbearable.

That's when I decided: I needed to change schools. But I couldn't just ask my parents without a good reason. It had to be something convincing. I could've just said I didn't like the school anymore, but that would never be enough. The truth was, I couldn't bear to face the memories of Pari. But I had to come up with something better.

I had one friend at school, my best friend, Anni. He was the only one who knew how much Pari meant to me, but I knew this decision would hurt him. He would be disappointed, but I couldn't stay there. I had to leave, for my own peace of mind.

I met Anni later that day and told him my plan. "Dude, I want to change schools," I said, trying to keep my voice steady.

"Why?" Anni asked, his brow furrowed in confusion.

"I can't study there. All those memories will haunt me," I replied, my voice barely above a whisper.

Anni shook his head. "Dude, you're just overreacting. It's not that bad."

But when it comes to love, there is no such thing as overreacting. You can't explain the pain of unspoken words, the ache of a love never confessed. It's something only those who have loved deeply can understand. And I was in that pain, unable to escape it.

Anni was upset, but he agreed to support me. It wasn't easy to convince him, but in the end, he understood. "We'll still hang out," I promised him. "We'll still be friends."

Now, I needed a solid reason to present to my parents. Anni didn't help much—he was too focused on his own feelings to think of a solution. But I was determined. I had to make it work.

That night, I went to my mom, who was chopping vegetables in the kitchen. I hesitated before speaking. "Mom, I want to learn something new. I want to learn Sanskrit."

She stopped chopping and looked at me, surprised. "What? Why?"

"I want to learn something that fewer people know," I replied, trying to sound convincing. The truth was, the school I wanted to transfer to offered Sanskrit as an elective, and my current school didn't. It was the perfect excuse, even if it was a lie.

My mom raised an eyebrow. "But school starts in three days. Why are you asking now?"

I knew convincing her wouldn't be easy, but I persisted. After a lot of pleading, she finally agreed to talk to my dad. My dad, on the other hand, was always more supportive of my decisions, no matter how strange they seemed. I went to him with the same request. At first, he didn't agree, but after a few minutes of convincing, he finally relented. He told me he would call around to see if any other schools had openings.

The next day, my dad made a few calls and, by some stroke of luck, found that one school had three seats left. I couldn't believe it. My dad told me he would go to my old school the next day to collect my Transfer Certificate (TC).

When he told me the news, I felt a strange sense of relief. At least now, I wouldn't have to face Pari. At least now, I could start fresh.

The next morning, my dad went to my old school to request my TC. The school administration told him that they needed me to come in person to sign the paperwork. I dreaded the thought of stepping foot in that place again, but there was no way around it. I had to go.

I walked through the gates of my old school, and as I did, I felt a rush of memories hit me. The laughter, the classrooms, the hallways where I had once hoped to confess my feelings to Pari—all of it felt like a lifetime ago. I tried to ignore the tightness in my chest as I made my way to the office.

"Why are you leaving?" a teacher asked as I signed the forms.

"I want to learn Sanskrit," I said, repeating the lie I had told my parents. It was the only reason I could give, and I stuck to it.

As I left the school for the last time, I felt a strange sense of finality. I wasn't just leaving the building; I was leaving behind a part of myself—the part that had once hoped for a future with Pari. That chapter of my life was over, and I had no choice but to turn the page.

I never went back to that school. And though I tried to bury the memories, there were times when they resurfaced, haunting me in the quiet moments. But I had made my decision. I had chosen to move on, even if the past would always linger in the background, like a shadow I could never quite outrun.

After countless signatures and paperwork, the process for my Transfer Certificate (TC) was finally completed. To collect it, I had to go to the clerk's office—the same place where I had once heard the most disturbing news of my life. That office felt like a gate to hell to me, a place where I could never escape the memories of my first love, Pari. But I had no choice. I had to go in to get the TC.

As I stepped inside, I began trembling, my heart pounding in my chest. I didn't understand why I felt this way, but the negativity of that place was overwhelming. Even now, when I think back to that office, it sends a chill down my spine.

I took a deep breath, trying to steady myself, and walked up to the desk. I signed the necessary forms as quickly as I could, then left the office as fast as possible, feeling the weight of the room's energy pressing down on me. After a few moments, the clerk came out to the waiting area and handed us the TC. It was done.

That same day, my parents and I went to the new school to complete my admission. The school was fine, I suppose, but I wasn't happy. I wasn't excited about the change, but I knew I had to leave my old school behind. Everyone has that one place they hate to go, and for me, that place was my school. It had become a constant reminder of what I had lost, and I needed to escape.

The new school was a big change. It was a high school, with classes ranging from 8th to 10th grade. The atmosphere was different—new environment, new friends, new teachers. I knew it would be hard for me to adjust. But the school had one thing that drew me in: Sanskrit. That's why I had transferred, after all. The school was known for promoting the language, and it was the only one in town that offered it.

On my first day, I walked into the classroom and immediately felt out of place. I didn't know anyone. Most of the students were from a different school, a smaller one that only offered classes up to 7th grade. They were all familiar with each other, and they were having fun, talking, and laughing together.

I, on the other hand, didn't feel like talking to anyone. I sat quietly in the corner of the bench, keeping to myself. As the days went by, I didn't open up to anyone. I acted like an introvert, withdrawing into myself. I had been such an active, playful kid at my old school, but now, I felt like a shadow of myself. I had stopped playing cricket—the sport I once loved, the one I had played to impress Pari. It felt like everything I had once enjoyed had been taken from me.

The days dragged on. I couldn't forget the memories of Pari. They constantly flashed through my mind, and no matter how hard I tried to move on, I couldn't. I didn't make any new friends at my new school. Anni was the only one left. We still met every evening to play, but even that felt different now.

Then, life threw another curveball at me. My grandmother had knee surgery, and since she lived in the village, she couldn't handle the busy city life anymore. My parents decided to move to a house on the outskirts of town, where she could recover in peace. The house was perfect for her—away from the hustle and bustle, surrounded by farms and fresh air. It was only about six kilometres from the city, so it wasn't too far from school, but it was in the opposite direction from our cricket ground.

I hated the idea of moving. Anni was the only friend I had left, and now, I was going to be even farther away from him. The new house was in a peaceful area, but it was also a long way from the only person I had left to talk to. My parents were excited about the move, but I wasn't.

When I told Anni about the move, he was furious. He thought I had somehow convinced my parents to change houses, but I explained the situation to him. After some convincing, he understood. I promised him that we would still meet up and play, but deep down, we both knew that things would never be the same.

At that time, social media wasn't as widespread, and data charges were high. We didn't have unlimited calling plans either. So, we made a pact: we would meet every weekend and during holidays, no matter what. I agreed, but in my heart, I knew that it wouldn't be the same.

After some renovations, our new house was ready. It was bigger than our old one, with a spacious terrace that offered a beautiful view of the surrounding hills and forests. The house was perfect for my grandmother, with plenty of space for her to walk around. But for me, it felt like a prison. I was leaving behind my childhood home—the place where I had grown up, the place where every corner held a memory.

There's a difference between a house and a home. A house is just a building, but a home is filled with family, laughter, and memories. It's the little things—the creaky windows, the broken locks, the table that always bumped when you walked by. It's the dark nights when the power goes out, and you can still navigate the rooms without bumping into anything because you've memorized every inch of the place.

Leaving that home was hard. It wasn't just a building to me; it was where I had spent my childhood. But I had no choice. I had to move.

The new house was nice. It was big and spacious, with a beautiful terrace and a view of the hills. The cold weather in the mornings was refreshing, and I loved the mist that covered the fields. The house was perfect for my grandmother, but for me, it was just a place I had to get used to.

I missed Anni. I missed the time we spent together, playing cricket, talking about life, and just being kids. Now, I was alone. My new school didn't have any friends for me, and I had no one to talk to. The days were long and lonely, with only school and home to fill them.

But my dad tried to make things better. Every day, after school, he would take me for a ride around the village or outside the city. We didn't have a destination; we just drove. He wanted me to get to know the area, to explore the places around our new home. He also taught me how to drive, letting me take the wheel on some of the village roads. At first, I didn't enjoy it, but after a while, I started to like it. There was something peaceful about driving through the countryside, with the mountains in the distance and the open road ahead of me.

But no matter how much I tried to adjust, I couldn't escape the feeling that something was missing. My life had changed in ways I couldn't control. The memories of Pari, the distance from Anni, and the isolation of my new home weighed heavily on me. I was trying to move on, to embrace this new chapter of my life, but the past kept haunting me, and I didn't know how to let go.

It was a Sunday, the kind of day that usually brought comfort and familiarity. My father had asked me to go on a long drive with him, as he often did on weekends. But this time, I had made a promise to Anni that we would meet every Sunday. So, I decided to ask my dad if Anni could come along. To my surprise, he agreed.

I called Anni, hoping he'd be up for the trip. But, as it turned out, he was going to some kind of ceremony with his parents, so he had to decline. It was the first weekend I had missed seeing him since moving to the new house. A wave of sadness washed over me, but deep down, I knew this would happen. Change was inevitable.

I informed my dad that Anni wouldn't be joining us and asked where we were headed. "Bengaluru," he replied. My heart skipped a beat. Bengaluru—such a vast city. The chances of seeing Pari there were almost non-existent, but something stirred within me. It was as if the universe was playing some kind of game with me. I had been trying so hard to forget her, yet now, when I least expected it, I found myself hoping, against all odds, that I might cross paths with her again.

I didn't know whether I was excited or nervous, happy, or sad. All I knew was that my emotions were a tangled mess. I had already agreed to the trip, and backing out now would make my dad suspicious. So, I forced myself to go along with it. It felt like destiny, or perhaps some cruel twist of fate, was bringing me closer to her in a way I hadn't anticipated.

I got ready quickly and, with a strange sense of anticipation, headed to the car. We left around 8 a.m. The journey to Bengaluru was about 350 kilometres, which would take roughly six hours. I had no idea where Pari lived in the city—only that she lived there somewhere. It felt like searching for a needle in a haystack, but still, I clung to a tiny sliver of hope.

As we drove, I couldn't help but look at every milestone along the way, each one bringing me a little closer to the city, and perhaps, to her. My dad, of course, wouldn't let me drive on the highway, so I passed the time by calculating how many kilometres we were from Bengaluru. The closer we got, the more excited I became. Even though I knew the chances of meeting her were slim, my heart refused to let go of the possibility. I kept telling myself that the chances were low, but they weren't zero.

Around 35% of the way into our journey, we stopped at a small roadside restaurant for food. My dad and I went inside, washed our hands, and sat at a table. He ordered a dosa, while I, in my curiosity, ordered something I had never tried before—Chow-chow bath. I had seen it on menus countless times but never thought to try it. When it arrived, I learned that Chow-chow bath was a combination of Upma and Kesari bath. Upma was a dish that everyone seemed to tolerate, but no one particularly liked. Kesari bath, on the other hand, was a sweet dish I could handle.

My dad couldn't help but laugh at me for not knowing what it was. "You didn't know what Chow-chow bath is?" he teased. I shrugged, embarrassed but amused. After finishing the meal, I bought some chocolates from a bakery outside the restaurant. I even bought two extra ones, just in case I ran into Pari. The thought seemed absurd, but I couldn't help it. I wanted to see her, to hug her tightly and tell her everything that had been weighing on my heart. I knew it was impossible, but I prayed to God that somehow, fate would lead me to her.

As we neared Bengaluru, the excitement in my chest grew. Only 20 kilometres to go. My heart raced with anticipation, and I couldn't help but feel like I was on the verge of something life-changing. But as we entered the city, that excitement was tempered by the reality that I might not see her at all. We reached the party hall where my dad's friend was hosting a small gathering. It was a business event, but to me, it felt like a waiting room for something more significant. My eyes scanned the room, hoping, praying that I would spot her.

But she wasn't there.

I tried to shake off the disappointment, telling myself it was foolish to expect anything. But deep down, my heart refused to accept the truth. The party was dull, and my dad was eager to introduce me to his business partners. He wanted me to learn the ins and outs of the business world, to understand whom to trust and whom not to. But all I could think about was Pari. I was so frustrated by my inability to find her. My brain understood that the chances of seeing her were almost zero, but my heart... my heart was stubborn, clinging to the hope that maybe, just maybe, I'd find her.

The party ended around 11:30 p.m., and my dad decided we would stay in a hotel for the night and head back in the morning. We checked in, and as my father fell asleep, I went to the window to look at the stars. The sky was beautiful, and the moon was almost full. It was a peaceful moment, but my mind wandered back to Pari. The memories of her, the times we spent together, flooded my thoughts. And then, without warning, a tear slipped down my cheek.

That night, I cried. Not because I had lost her, but because I had never fully let go. It was the first time in a long while that I allowed myself to feel the weight of it all. I cried quietly, not wanting my father to hear. Boys don't cry, they say. But sometimes, crying is the only way to release the pain that lingers in your chest. It's a silent therapy, a way to heal. The next morning, my father found me asleep at the window sill, and he gently moved me to the bed. He didn't know what I had been going through, and I didn't want him to.

After breakfast, we checked out of the hotel, and on the way back, I opened the complimentary hamper the hotel had given us. Inside were chocolates, dry fruits, and a small bottle of perfume. I picked up the perfume and opened the cap, inhaling the fragrance. The smell hit me like a wave, and for a moment, I was transported back to the times I spent with Pari. Her hair, her scent—it was all so vivid in my mind. The perfume smelled just like her hair, and I couldn't help but feel the familiar ache in my chest.

Every mile we drove away from Bengaluru felt like a mile farther from her. The closer we got to home, the more the pain intensified. The memories, the scent, the hope—it all lingered. And I realized, sometimes, the smallest things—the scent of a perfume, the sound of a song, the sight of a place—can bring back memories you thought you had buried. Distance, too, hurts. But sometimes, the people we love are meant to be loved from afar.

And as the miles between us grew, I understood that the heart will always carry the love it cannot let go of, no matter how far it travels.

6
Whispers of Second Chance...

The cry that day, sitting on the window sill, marked a pivotal moment in my journey. That was when I truly began moving on. Though the fragrance of the perfume I had smelled earlier on the trip to Bengaluru brought back memories of Pari, I was able to control the wave of emotions that surged within me. Slowly, the part of me that had been struggling to let go started to ease.

When I returned from Bengaluru, my routine resumed. School was the same—going alone, coming back alone. Weekends, once filled with time spent with Anni, had become quieter. Anni and I hadn't been meeting as much. I wasn't sure why, but the small distance between us seemed to be widening. It was tough, but I couldn't force things to go back to how they were.

It had been around three months since I joined the new school, but I still didn't feel fully connected. Some of the students were friendly enough, but I didn't feel the camaraderie I had hoped for. It felt like they were just talking to me because they had to, not because they genuinely wanted to.

Then, something unexpected happened. We had an NCC (National Cadet Corps) selection at school. Initially, I wasn't too interested, but I figured it would be a good way to escape class for a while. Plus, there was a 10-day camp next year, which I thought would be fun. So, I went along, not really expecting anything.

The selection process was tough. Many students from our section showed up, lured by the promise of free attendance for any NCC-related events. But there were strict eligibility criteria—mainly height and weight—and most of the boys from our section were rejected. Out of the 30 students who had shown up, only five passed the eligibility check. Then, there was the physical test: a run around the entire school ground, three laps. The first 20 to finish would be selected.

I made it through. But it wasn't easy. Only four of us from my section passed, and I found myself growing closer to Jai, one of the other boys who had made it through. He was new to the school, just like me, and didn't have many friends either. But he was outgoing, especially with the girls, and although he was always chatting with them, he spent time with me as well. Over time, we formed a small bond, but it was nothing like the deep friendship I had hoped for.

As days passed, life felt monotonous. Anni and I were no longer meeting as often, and I felt a subtle shift in our relationship. I didn't know exactly what had caused it, but the distance between us had crept in slowly, and I couldn't reverse it.

The final exams were approaching, and I found myself struggling. I wasn't motivated to study. Back in the days when Pari was still part of my life, I had studied hard, driven by the desire to impress her. That had been my fuel, and it had worked. I had always been an average student, but I had managed to get good marks. Now, without that motivation, my grades slipped. I barely managed to scrape through the exams.

My parents noticed the change in me. They asked about my new school, about whether I had made any friends. But I hadn't mentioned a single friend to them. I simply said everything was fine, but they could tell something was off. To distract them, I invited Anni over to our new home. I knew his visit would make both my parents and me happy. It was the first time in a while that I felt a spark of joy.

Summer came, and I decided to visit my grandparents. I had always enjoyed spending time with them, but now, with the chaos of school and life, I found that I looked forward to their house more than ever. I spent a week there, and after that, we all planned a family trip to Goa and Dandeli.

By the time the trip came around, I had almost completely moved on from Pari. I enjoyed the family vacation, forcing myself to let go of the past and embrace the present. It was refreshing to be away from the monotony of school and the weight of unspoken feelings.

The holidays flew by, and soon it was time to return to school. The first day back was filled with the usual hustle and bustle. We had an NCC meeting that day, and I learned that we would be going on a 10-day camp in Mysuru. I was thrilled. Ten days away from school sounded like a dream, especially with the other students stuck in class. Little did I know, the camp would turn out to be far more gruelling than I had imagined.

The camp began with an early wake-up call at 5 a.m., followed by physical exercises and parades until noon. In the afternoon, we had theory classes. It was tough, but I was determined to push through. I thought it would help me build strength, both physically and mentally. But little did I know, destiny had more in store for me than I had anticipated.

As the days counted down to the camp, I began to feel unwell. I was constantly tired, and my health deteriorated rapidly. Three days before the camp, I had a high fever, but I still decided to go. I was weak, but I didn't want to miss the opportunity.

The day before the camp, I packed my things, feeling only half of my usual energy. I had to buy a few last-minute items like shampoo and soap for the trip. Despite my condition, I was determined to go.

The next morning, I woke up early, got ready, and my dad dropped me off at school. We gathered at 5:30 a.m., and the bus to Mysuru was waiting. But the other students weren't there yet. Gradually, they started showing up, and soon enough, we were ready to board. Only 15 cadets were going from our school, and Jai and I were the only two from my section.

Jai, as usual, was late. The rest of the group had to wait for him, and when he finally arrived, he scanned the bus for a seat. I had saved one for him next to me.

The first 10 minutes of the journey were awkwardly silent, but I broke the ice by asking Jai why he was late. He explained that he had lost his socks and was searching for a new pair. I couldn't help but smile at his answer, and soon enough, we were chatting away. As the bus rumbled down the road, most of the other students were still sleepy, but Jai and I kept talking.

Eventually, Jai drifted off to sleep, but I couldn't. I never could sleep while traveling. I always enjoyed the journey more than the destination. There was something about the road, the changing scenery, the quiet hum of the bus, that always kept me awake.

"Sometimes, journeys are more beautiful than destinations," I thought to myself as I gazed out of the window, watching the world blur by.

So, I started to look outside the window, letting my gaze wander across the landscape. The roads stretched out before us, winding through the lush greenery of the Western Ghats. It was June, the beginning of the monsoon season, and the air was crisp and cool. The gentle breeze swept across the empty paddy fields, which had already been ploughed and were now ready for the new crops. In the middle of these fields, the paddy seedlings stood tall, waiting to be planted. As the morning breeze passed through them, they seemed to dance, their delicate green tips swaying in rhythm with the wind.

Birds were darting through the sky, eager to gather food before the heavy rains arrived. Farmers had placed scarecrows around the seedlings, hoping to deter the mischievous birds from stealing the young plants. The scene was peaceful, the natural beauty of the land unfolding in front of me. The early monsoons in the Western Ghats, known as Malenadu or Malnad in Kannada, were as magnificent as the name suggested—"land of rain" or "place of the mountain range." The landscape was alive with colour, the mountains and valleys wrapped in a misty embrace.

We cruised through the winding village roads, and I could feel the landscape shifting as we neared the highway. The vibrant green fields gave way to more developed areas, and the raw beauty of nature began to fade, replaced by the more structured, urban landscape.

As we approached the highway, we stopped at a small roadside hotel for breakfast. Everyone was hungry after the long journey, and the food gave us all a much-needed energy boost. It was like a switch had been flipped. Suddenly, the bus was filled with energy. Laughter and chatter filled the air, and a few of the cadets started to suggest playing music and dancing to pass the time.

I was in the mood to join in. I had already moved on from my one-sided relationship with Pari, and now I was ready to embrace the carefree energy I had once admired in Parth, my old schoolmate. I wanted to feel free, to dance without a care in the world. So, I decided to let go of my reservations and join the others.

We all piled back into the bus, and I asked the driver to play some upbeat rock music. He complied, and soon the bus was alive with music. The Kannada songs pumped through the speakers, and for the next 40 minutes, everyone danced and sang along. But eventually, the energy began to wane. People were tired again, and the excitement faded. I, however, wasn't ready to stop. I wanted to dance more, to keep the energy alive, but no one seemed to have the same enthusiasm.

The driver, noticing the shift in mood, changed the playlist to a series of slow, melancholic breakup songs. The lively atmosphere quickly turned subdued. Most of the cadets sat quietly, talking amongst themselves. Jai, who had been chatting earlier, fell asleep again. I, on the other hand, returned to staring out of the window. For some reason, I felt content. It was a strange feeling, one that I couldn't quite explain, but I welcomed it.

The weather that day was neither too sunny nor too cloudy. The wind carried a chill, hinting at the rain that was falling somewhere in the distance. As we continued on our journey, the sky darkened, and the first few drops of rain began to fall. The drizzle was light at first, but it soon picked up, and the bus windows were quickly shut to keep the rain out.

I, however, left my window slightly open. I wanted to inhale the fresh, earthy aroma that would fill the air when the first raindrops hit the parched earth. The soil, heated by the sun for months, would absorb the first drop of rain and then release a fragrance that would fill the atmosphere. It was a smell I had always loved, and I didn't want to miss it. As the rain began to fall more heavily, I closed my eyes for a moment, savouring the scent that seemed to make the whole world feel more alive.

We still had about 100 kilometres left to reach our destination, and the rain made the journey even more special. By the time we reached Mysuru around 1 p.m., the sky had cleared a little, and the sun was peeking through the clouds. As we entered the security gate of the university campus, I couldn't help but marvel at the sight. The entire campus was surrounded by trees and flowers, and the university seemed more like a forest than an academic institution. There was a narrow path between the trees that led to the hostel where we would be staying for the next 10 days.

We passed through the security gate and proceeded to report our arrival at the camp. The camp staff took our names, addresses, biometric fingerprints, and pupil prints before handing us the keys to our rooms. There were only three rooms allocated for the cadets, and since there were 15 of us, that meant five cadets per room. Jai and I, along with three other boys from a different section, would share a room. We knew them by face, but we weren't close friends.

After settling into our rooms and freshening up, it was around 5 p.m. The orientation program was scheduled to begin at 6 p.m., so we decided to take an hour to explore the campus. Mysuru was a green and clean city, and the university reflected that. The campus was well-maintained, with lush gardens and trees that seemed to stretch on forever. After walking around for a while, we headed toward the seminar hall for the orientation.

As we walked, I passed a tree and felt a spider web brush against my face. The ticklish sensation made me stop and rub my face to clear the web away. As I did, I remembered something I had once seen in a cartoon. In Japan and Thailand, it was believed that walking through a spider web meant you would meet a new friend that day. I chuckled at the thought, dismissing it as a silly omen. I didn't believe in such things, but I couldn't help wondering if it was a coincidence.

We continued walking, and as we approached the seminar hall, something strange happened. A girl hurried past me, and although I didn't get a good look at her, I had this sudden, inexplicable feeling that I knew her. I stopped for a moment, trying to catch a glimpse of her face, but she was already gone. My curiosity was piqued, but I didn't have time to think about it. Jai, who was walking behind me, asked what had happened, but I just shrugged it off. "Nothing," I said, though I couldn't shake the feeling.

We entered the seminar hall, where we were assigned seats. The orientation program was about to begin, and we were all instructed to leave our phones in the hostel room. I had managed to sneak a pack of chewing gum into my pocket, so that was our only hope for passing the time.

The program started, and the camp organizers asked for volunteers to sing a prayer. A group of cadets stood up and sang, and after they were finished, the organizers thanked them before launching into the long, tedious speech. I could feel my eyelids growing heavy. The travel, combined with the lack of sleep during the journey, had taken its toll. I had barely slept on the bus, and now, in the quiet seminar hall, I struggled to stay awake. Before long, I had drifted off to sleep, the sound of the speaker's voice fading into the background as I succumbed to exhaustion.

That day, something happened that I didn't even notice because I had fallen asleep. During the orientation speech, the speaker noticed that some students seemed bored, so he called a girl up to the stage to sing. The moment she began, I missed it entirely. I was too deep in my slumber, but I heard the others around me talking about her afterward. Everyone was praising her voice, saying how beautiful it was, but I hadn't heard a single note.

After the program ended, we headed to the dining hall for dinner. The atmosphere had lightened, and everyone was talking and laughing. Once we finished eating, Jai and I decided to go for a walk around the campus. I threw on my hoodie, and we wandered through the quiet paths, discussing movies and songs. Jai was especially fond of all the Avengers films and English movies in general. I'd watched some of them too, so our conversation flowed easily.

As we walked, a sudden gust of wind swept through the trees, sending leaves scattering all around us. Some leaves landed on me and Jai, but one leaf got caught in the cap of my hoodie. I didn't notice it, and we continued walking, oblivious to the small change in my appearance.

Then, out of nowhere, I heard a voice.

"Excuse me…"

The voice cut through the air, and something in me froze. It wasn't just the sound of her voice; it was the way it reached me. The sound seemed to bypass my ears and go straight to my heart, a familiar tug that I couldn't explain. Everything around me went silent—no more background music, no more rustling leaves, nothing. It was as if the world had paused, and all I could hear was that voice. It was unmistakable.

I knew that voice. It was Pari's.

Though it had been years, and though her voice might have changed slightly with time and age, I recognized it instantly. It was the same tone, the same accent, the same warmth that had once filled my days. A chill ran through me, and for a moment, I couldn't move. My body felt paralyzed, like it didn't belong to me anymore.

Jai, who was walking beside me, didn't seem as affected. He turned around first, probably wondering why I had stopped so suddenly. When he saw her, he didn't seem to react the way I did.

I hesitated, but then I slowly turned toward the voice. And there she was—Pari.

As soon as I laid eyes on her, memories flooded my mind. The time we spent together, her laugh, the way her eyes would sparkle when she smiled, the feeling of her hand in mine. I remembered everything, all at once. Her eyes, dark and wide, framed by the kajal she used to wear. They reminded me of grapes floating in milk, so dark and deep. Her smile, like an eclipse, always lighting up the room. I could almost hear her laughter, so light and carefree. All of it came rushing back, in a heartbeat.

But I didn't know what to say. I was frozen, my voice trembling. I just stood there, looking at her, unable to speak. Jai, ever the practical one, broke the silence.

"Yeah, there's a leaf stuck in his hoodie's cap," Jai said, pointing to the leaf that was still caught in my hoodie.

Pari smiled and gently removed the leaf from my cap. I couldn't even bring myself to say thank you at first, but I managed to find my voice.

"Thank you," I said, my voice barely above a whisper.

She smiled at me, a familiar, warm smile that made my heart skip a beat. "Hey, you're Partha, right?"

Jai looked at me in surprise, clearly not recognizing her. He didn't know who she was. I hadn't mentioned Pari to him yet. We weren't that close, and I hadn't felt the need to bring her up. Besides, I had already moved on. I didn't want to revisit the past.

"Yeah, you remember?" I replied, trying to sound casual, though my heart was racing.

Pari's smile widened, and she looked at me with a mix of nostalgia and warmth. "How could I forget? You were one of my best friends in class. And you had one of the coolest aquariums I've ever seen."

I smiled, though my heart was still thundering in my chest. I tried to act normal, as if this was just another random encounter, but it wasn't. It was Pari, and after all these years, I hadn't expected to see her again, let alone have a conversation like this. But I played it cool, trying to keep my composure.

Pari was with a girl I didn't recognize. She was staring at me, not just glancing, but staring, as if trying to figure me out. It made me feel a little awkward, and I didn't know how to continue the conversation. The silence stretched between us, thick and uncomfortable.

Finally, Pari broke it with a smile. "Well, I guess I'll see you around. Bye!" she said, waving.

I smiled, a little too quickly. "Bye," I replied, my voice shaky.

The whole interaction had lasted only a minute, but it felt like an eternity. As soon as she walked away, my mind was racing. I couldn't stop thinking about what had just happened. I had been doing so well, moving on, focusing on the present. But now, after seeing her again, everything felt like it had been turned upside down.

Jai, who had been scrolling through his phone while I talked to Pari, didn't ask me about her. I think he had figured out who she was through our conversation. He knew she was from my old school, but he didn't pry.

We continued walking in silence, heading back toward our rooms. Everyone was tired from the long day of travel, and the camp activities had drained us. As soon as we reached the room, we all collapsed into bed. I was exhausted, but sleep didn't come easily. My mind was still racing, and Pari's face kept flashing in front of my eyes.

I had already been tired, having not slept during the journey, and now, even as I lay in bed, I couldn't fall asleep. My mind kept replaying the moment when I saw her again.

It was like I was standing at the edge of moving on, ready to leave the past behind. If I had made it through this camp without seeing her, I might have been able to finally let go. But fate had other plans. Destiny had decided to reintroduce Pari into my life, even if only for a brief moment.

As I lay there, my heart conflicted between the desire to love her again and the knowledge of the pain she had caused me when she left the city.

Some people say, "Things never happen the same way twice," but that day, it felt like they had. When I saw her again, it was as if I was seeing her for the first time. The way

I felt, the way my heart raced—it was just like it had been back then.

I realized that the reason I had liked her so much was because she had been my first in so many ways. She was the first person I had ever wanted to spend more time with in class, the first person who made me care about getting good marks, the first person I had ever imagined spending my life with. It might seem like a small thing now, but back then, it had been everything.

And even though I had moved on, even though I had convinced myself that I was over her, seeing her again had stirred something deep inside me. Something I wasn't sure I was ready to face again.

I was stuck in a state of confusion, torn between two opposite emotions that clashed within me. I wasn't sure how to feel anymore. The night had left me restless, my thoughts swirling in a storm I couldn't escape. Deep down, I felt like I didn't deserve to be loved. It was as if the weight of my past had made me unworthy of any future happiness. I wanted to walk away from everything, to lose myself in the emptiness and try to fill the gaps in my life on my own. I knew I shouldn't listen to the voice inside my head in the dead of night, but sometimes, those voices become so loud, so persistent, that it's hard to ignore them. And deep down, I knew they were telling me the truth, even if I didn't want to accept it.

I wished, though, that she knew how I felt—how I had felt when I first saw her, how my heart had raced when our eyes met, how I had longed for her to stay with me, to share a life together. But those were just wishes, and I knew they were never meant to be fulfilled. The reality was different now, and no amount of longing could change that.

I tried to rewrite my story, to push her out of the narrative, to move on without her. But even as I did, I knew there would always be a blank space, a missing chapter that I couldn't fill. Blank pages were better than torn ones, I reminded myself, but that didn't make the emptiness any easier to bear.

To be honest, there was a part of me that would always hold onto her, a small corner of my heart where my feelings for her would remain hidden. It would stay buried deep within me, only surfacing when I chose to remember her. But for now, I decided to bury those feelings, to act like nothing had happened. I knew it would be difficult, but I made up my mind to do it. I had to move on.

The next morning, everyone woke up at 4:30 a.m. I hadn't slept at all, and the exhaustion hit me hard. My eyes were swollen from the lack of rest, and I could barely keep my focus. But I had no choice. The morning exercise was mandatory. I dragged myself out of bed, freshened up, and joined the others for the workout.

Jai noticed the change in me right away. "Are you alright?" he asked, his voice laced with concern.

"I'm fine," I replied, though I knew he could tell something was off. He didn't press me, though. We went through the warm-up routine, and then the trainer arrived, instructing us to run three laps around the campus—around 7 kilometres in total. Everyone groaned at the announcement. We all knew the camp was going to be tough, but none of us had expected the first session to be this intense.

The running began, and while everyone else was struggling, I was determined to push through. I wanted to tire myself out completely, to reach a point where my body was too exhausted to think about anything else. I needed to clear my mind, to stop the storm of emotions that had been swirling in my head.

I started running faster than everyone else, my legs moving in a blur. But since we had to run in a line, I slowed down to match the pace of the others. The boys and girls were trained separately, as the girls had different physical limitations, and the exercises were adjusted accordingly.

As we ran past a field where the girls were doing aerobics, I couldn't help but feel a wave of frustration. Their exercises looked so much easier than ours, and the boys grumbled amongst themselves about the unfairness of it. But no one dared to question the trainers. The trainers were all from the army, and asking questions could lead to punishment—things like 30 dips or rolling in gravel for five minutes. No one wanted to deal with that, so we kept our complaints to ourselves and finished the run in silence.

Afterward, the session was dismissed, and we headed back for a quick shower and breakfast. The food wasn't great, but it was healthy and full of protein, which was good for our bodies. We got ready for the parade practice, which wasn't too difficult. We just had to march in formation for a few hours. By the time we finished, it was already afternoon.

Lunch followed, and while it wasn't the most flavourful meal, it was enough to fill us up. The physical activity had worked up our appetites, and we ate without complaint. After lunch, we had a theory class. But after all the exertion, most of us were too tired to pay attention. The thick, creamy curd they served us only made things worse, putting everyone into a food coma. Some of the students even banged their heads against the benches as they dozed off, the loud thud echoing in the otherwise quiet room.

Finally, at 4 o'clock, the class ended, and we were free for a short break. We had coffee and cookies, and then we headed back to our rooms, thinking we could relax for a while. But just when we thought the day was over, we were told that there was an entertainment session in the evening. It was mandatory, of course—movies and drama performances that we had to attend.

At 7 o'clock sharp, we were required to assemble in the conference hall. By the time we got there, all the seats on the boys' side were taken, so we had to sit behind the girls. The others were excited, and some of the boys even looked jealous. But I wasn't excited. In fact, I was dreading it. I didn't want to see Pari again. Everything felt like it was happening against my will, as if fate had decided to throw her back into my life at the most inconvenient time.

I sat as far from the front as I could, in the back corner of the hall, hoping to avoid seeing her. But fate wasn't done with me yet. Pari was already assigned to perform three acts that night, and the first one was a prayer song. She stood on stage with her group, and as soon as I heard her voice, it felt like my heart stopped.

I had already prepared myself to remain indifferent, to act like I didn't care, but hearing her sing was one of the hardest things I'd ever done. Everyone around me was enjoying the performance, but I sat there, stone-faced, trying not to react. It took every ounce of my willpower to get through the entire program without showing any emotion.

After the performance, we filed out of the hall and headed back to our rooms. As we walked, I overheard some boys from my school, but from a different section, talking about Pari. They were complimenting her and arguing about who would get to flirt with her.

A wave of anger surged through me. My hands trembled, and my body shook with rage. I wanted to lash out, to confront those boys and tell them to leave her alone. But I held myself back. Since Pari had left me, I had become short-tempered, snapping at the smallest things. I didn't know if it was because of my puberty or the emotional pain of losing her, but either way, I was quick to anger now. And hearing those boys talk about her like that made something inside me snap.

I tried to push the anger away, but it lingered, festering in my chest. I knew I had to move on, but every time I heard her name, every time I saw her, it felt like I was falling backward into the past, unable to escape the feelings I had buried so deep.

The boys talking about her was like pouring gasoline onto a burning fire. My anger flared up instantly, and my body trembled with rage. But I didn't let it show. I forced myself to remain calm, to keep my emotions in check. I knew that if I started caring less, it would be easier to move on. But sometimes, letting go of thoughts isn't as easy as it seems. As the saying goes, *Love is not something you forget immediately. It's something that stays with you, even when you try not to think about it.*

I still loved her, even though I knew she was like the moon—beautiful and distant, something I could never reach. She was the warmth my heart craved, but one I could never truly have. I still loved her, even though I understood she would always remain an incomplete chapter in my life. There were millions of reasons why I should stop thinking about her, reasons that I tried to convince myself were valid. But there was one powerful reason that kept me bound to her: Love.

I never knew what it felt like to be loved in return, but I wanted to be her first choice. I wanted to be the main character in her story. I wanted to be the wallpaper on her phone, the initials she wrote on her palm with henna. I wanted to be the first person she thought of in the morning and the last person she thought of before she fell asleep. I longed for those simple, beautiful moments. But time and destiny were not on my side.

I still hoped that she would come to me in my dreams, that her presence there would be enough to satisfy my heart. But instead, she became the reason I couldn't sleep at all. I couldn't even dream unless I fell asleep, and my thoughts of her were the only thing keeping me awake.

All these feelings were swirling in my mind, and I knew I had to focus on what I had come to the camp for—to move on.

The next day, I woke up and went through my daily routine. I joined the others for the parade practice, and as usual, I saw her. She looked at me and waved, and I simply smiled back before continuing with the task at hand.

Later that evening, as I went for my usual walk, I saw Pari and her friends again. This time, I didn't want to talk to her. I had already made up my mind to avoid her, so I asked Jai to walk on the other side. As the days passed, I started avoiding her more and more. It wasn't easy, and I wondered why it was so difficult. Then, I realized that it wasn't just about forgetting the past or avoiding her in the present—it was about letting go of the small wish I had of spending my future with her.

Finally, it was the last day of the camp. There were no intense activities planned, just a small program where they would distribute certificates to everyone who had participated. After lunch, there was a closing ceremony, which turned out to be longer than expected, lasting until 6:30 p.m. Afterward, we returned to our rooms to freshen up before heading to dinner.

As usual, Jai and I went for a walk afterward. The weather was cloudy and windy, so I put on my jacket and plugged in my earphones. Jai wasn't as interested in walking, so we decided to cut it short and head back. But then, I heard someone calling my name. I turned around, and to my surprise, it was Pari, walking toward me with three of her friends.

I pulled out my earphones and looked at her, confused. Why was she calling me? After all the days of avoiding her, I didn't understand why she was suddenly reaching out to me. Jai, noticing what was happening, nodded toward the room, signalling that he would head back without me. I gave him a thumbs-up, signalling that I would join him later.

As I walked toward her, I noticed that she had told her friends to go back. She was the only one walking toward me. My heart began to race. Why was she coming to talk to me alone? Why had she sent her friends away? My mind raced with questions, but I kept walking, unsure of what to expect.

"Hi," Pari said, her voice a little hesitant.

"Hello," I replied, trying to keep my composure.

"Can I ask you something?" she asked, her tone curious but tinged with something else. I felt my nerves spike. I didn't know what was coming, but I knew it would be important.

"Yeah," I replied, my voice barely above a whisper.

"Are we not friends anymore?" she asked, her eyes searching mine for an answer.

"Yeah, we are," I said, but even as I spoke, I felt a pang of guilt. It wasn't that simple.

"But I don't feel like we're friends anymore," she continued, her voice growing more frustrated. "You've been avoiding me for days, like we're enemies or something. I've been noticing it for the past eight days. When I first saw you at the camp, I was so happy to find a friend I was close with. But after that day, when you said hello, you stopped talking to me. Even when I tried to talk to you, you didn't seem interested."

She kept talking, not giving me a chance to respond. Her words were like arrows, piercing through the silence that had built up between us. I could see the frustration in her eyes, the hurt in her voice. I wanted to say something, to explain, but the words wouldn't come. All I could do was listen.

As she spoke, I couldn't help but notice the way her eyes flashed with emotion. I could feel the weight of her words, even without them being fully articulated. Her lips moved quickly, but all I could focus on was the depth of her gaze. She was angry, yes, but there was something else—something I couldn't quite place.

Suddenly, she stopped, and the silence between us felt like a thousand years. It was my turn to speak, but I didn't know where to begin. I could feel the weight of everything I wanted to say, but the words were trapped inside me.

"I'm sorry," I finally said, my voice barely audible.

"It's not about an apology," she replied quickly, her tone softening slightly. "If we had talked, we could have remembered the good times from school. It would have been fun."

I stood there, silently, watching her. She continued, her words flowing out in a steady stream.

"It's okay," she said, her voice quieter now. "Next time you see me, talk to me. Please don't make it awkward."

"Okay," I said, nodding.

"Bye, then," she said, offering a small smile as she extended her hand. I smiled back, but I didn't say anything. I didn't know what to say. She smiled again, turned, and walked away, heading toward her room.

As I stood there, I realized that this might be the last time I would ever see her. My heart felt heavy with the unspoken words, the things I had wanted to say but couldn't. I wondered if I had made a mistake by not talking to her sooner, by keeping my distance when all she wanted was a friend.

She had been lonely, struggling to find her place in this unfamiliar world, and she thought that talking to an old friend would make things better. But for me, it wasn't that simple. The silence between us wasn't because I had nothing to say—it was because there was so much, I needed to say, and I couldn't bring myself to speak it.

When she asked if we were still friends, I wanted to tell her that I was more than just a friend to her. I wanted to tell her that, for me, she was everything. But the words never came.

As I watched her walk away, I felt the weight of her absence pressing down on me. I missed her eyes, the sparkle in them when she laughed, the sound of her voice. I missed the way she made everything feel lighter, the way she brought a sense of joy to even the simplest conversations.

I wanted to go back to the days when everything felt normal, when I didn't know she would be leaving. But time had already passed, and the moments we had shared were now just memories.

I began to walk back to my room, my heart heavy with regret. I knew I had done something wrong, that I should have said goodbye properly. But it was too late now. The possibility of seeing her again seemed non-existent. The last memory I had of her couldn't be imperfect.

I stopped in my tracks and turned around. "Pari!" I shouted, my voice breaking through the silence.

She turned back, a surprised look on her face.

"I'm sorry," I shouted, the words tumbling out. "Goodbye."

She smiled at me, that same warm smile I would always remember, and then she turned and walked away.

I stood there for a moment, feeling a sense of relief wash over me. The conversation had been incomplete, but in its own way, it felt complete. It was imperfect, but it was perfect in its imperfection.

As I walked back to my room, a single tear escaped from my eye. It was a tear of sadness, of love unspoken, of a story that would never have a conclusion. But sometimes, it's better to leave things with a little twist, a little mystery.

To get something you've never had, you have to do something you've never done. I didn't have the courage to confess my feelings, and I didn't want to hurt her again by telling her the truth. The story of us would never have a clear ending. And maybe, just maybe, that was okay.

I went to the bathroom and washed my face, hoping to clear the heaviness I felt inside. The cool water on my skin was refreshing, but it didn't ease the ache in my heart. I walked back to the room, avoiding eye contact with Jai. He looked up from his phone and asked, "Are you okay?"

I gave a weak smile, trying to reassure him. "Yeah, I'm fine," I replied, though the words didn't feel real. I climbed into my bed and pulled the blanket over me, trying to bury myself in the warmth. But my mind wouldn't let me rest. I turned toward the window beside my bed, where the faint sound of raindrops tapping against the glass echoed in the room. The wind howled outside, and the door of the window rattled with each gust. I could see the trees near the streetlight swaying in the wind, their branches dancing in the storm.

Suddenly, memories of all the moments we had shared together flooded my mind—the laughter, the conversations, the quiet glances. A small smile tugged at the corners of my lips, but it was bittersweet. A tear, which had been struggling not to fall, finally broke free and traced a path down my cheek. It was strange. The pain in my heart was still there, but in that moment, I felt an odd sense of peace.

That night, I slept better than I had in days. I didn't wake up once, and for the first time during the entire camp, I felt truly at ease. The pain was still there, but somehow, it didn't feel as overwhelming. I woke up at 5 a.m., feeling refreshed and more at peace than I had been in a long time. There was a certain charm in my face that I couldn't quite explain. It was as if, for a brief moment, I had found some clarity.

We were scheduled to leave at 6:30 a.m. to head back to our hometown. I quickly got dressed, and as I finished getting ready, I could hear the bus outside. The boys had already gathered, and they all claimed the same seats they had sat in on the way to the camp. I found my seat and sat down, feeling a strange sense of finality in the air.

A few minutes later, Jai came over and sat next to me. Over the past ten days, our bond had grown stronger. We had spent so much time together that I could sense his concern when he looked at me. He didn't say anything at first, but I could feel his eyes on me.

"Are you okay?" he asked quietly.

I nodded, though I wasn't entirely sure myself. "Yeah, I'm fine," I muttered, but I didn't meet his gaze.

Jai patted my shoulder. "No, you're not. I know something's bothering you. You weren't yourself last night."

I hesitated. He was right. I had been distant, lost in my own thoughts. But I didn't want to talk about it. Not yet.

"Do you like her?" Jai asked, his voice casual but probing.

"Who?" I asked, trying to play it off.

"The girl from last night. The one you were talking to."

I felt a lump form in my throat, and I turned my head to look out the window, trying to avoid his gaze. "No," I said quickly, hoping to end the conversation.

Jai raised an eyebrow, clearly unconvinced. "Don't lie to me, dude. I can tell something's bothering you. I don't know you for long, but I can see it. You're not fooling anyone."

I stayed silent, staring out the window at the passing scenery. Jai wasn't going to let it go. He asked again, his voice softer this time, but still insistent.

"Do you like her?"

I sighed, the weight of the truth finally pressing on me. "Yeah, I do. In fact, I love her," I admitted, my voice barely above a whisper.

Jai didn't say anything at first. I could feel his eyes on me, waiting for me to say more. "Did you tell her how you feel?" he asked, his tone gentle.

"No," I replied, shaking my head. "I can't. I'm not good enough for her. I'm not the one she deserves. She deserves better."

As soon as the words left my mouth, I could feel the moisture in my eyes. It wasn't just the rain outside. My eyes were welling up, the weight of my emotions too much to bear. Jai noticed immediately. He didn't say anything, but I could see the sympathy in his eyes.

"Chill, Partha," Jai said, his voice soft but comforting. "It's okay. You'll get through this." He patted my shoulder again and gave me a side hug, a gesture of support that I didn't know I needed until that moment.

I nodded, but I didn't say anything in return. I didn't know how to respond. I was still trying to process everything. The conversation was over for now, but the truth of my feelings hung in the air like a heavy fog.

I put my earphones in and closed my eyes, trying to block out the thoughts that were swirling in my mind. The bus ride felt different this time. It wasn't just the destination that mattered—it was the journey. The destination was my home, but in that moment, I was just trying to find peace within myself.

As the bus continued its journey, I looked out the window one last time. The rain had stopped, but the clouds still hung low in the sky. The world outside felt quieter, as if everything was waiting for something. The trees swayed gently in the breeze, and I couldn't help but think of her—the way she had looked at me, the way her voice had sounded, the way everything had felt when we were together.

But now, all I could do was move forward. The camp was over, and it was time to go back to the reality I had left behind. The pain in my chest was still there, but it didn't feel as sharp as it had before. Maybe, in time, it would fade. Maybe not. But for now, I had to focus on what was ahead.

Jai leaned back in his seat, and I did the same. We didn't need to talk anymore. The silence between us felt comfortable, like an unspoken understanding. We were both lost in our own thoughts, but we were no longer alone.

And as the bus rolled down the road, I realized that sometimes, the journey itself is just as important as the destination.

7
New Old Life...

The camp hadn't gone as I had planned. Everything took a different turn, and while the camp itself was enjoyable, I was too distracted to fully immerse myself in the experience. But by the end of the final day, I had completely moved on. Sometimes, when I thought back on those days, a pang of sadness would hit me, but I was okay with it. As the saying goes, *"The soul always knows what to do to heal itself; the challenge is to silence the mind."* I was trying my best to silence my mind, but the glimpses of her would always sneak back into my thoughts. Yet, it was alright. After all, *we can't get a rainbow without a little rain.*

Things were starting to feel like they were falling into place. The pressure of the board exams loomed over me, and with that came the decision of which stream to choose for my future. I needed to focus on my studies.

Jai and I had become best friends after the camp. The void that Anni had left was slowly being filled by him. I had lost touch with Anni over time, and the communication had become increasingly difficult. We didn't have our own cell phones, and social media wasn't as prevalent then. Our interactions had become sporadic, and we only met once every few months.

Before I knew it, high school was over in the blink of an eye, and the board exams were upon us. Everyone was focused on studying, and I was no different. However, my dedication to my studies wasn't the same as when I was trying to impress Pari. The pressure during exam time was immense—not from my parents, who were pretty chill about it—but from relatives. They constantly called, reminding me to focus on my studies, to get good marks, and to choose the science stream.

I did my best, and I managed to get good grades—not excellent, but good enough to secure a spot in the science stream. My parents, thinking it was the best option for me, enrolled me in one of the best colleges in town for my pre-university (PU) studies.

I wasn't entirely happy with their decision. I had wanted to go outside the town, but the thought of missing home made me hesitate. It felt like I was stuck between a rock and a hard place. Either option seemed difficult. In the end, I went along with my parents' choice, thinking it would make them happy and, at least, I wouldn't miss home. It wasn't a win-win situation, but it was the best I could do.

So, I joined the college in town, which was known for being strict—both in terms of academics and extracurricular activities. Making new friends would be hard, especially since Jai had already joined a college outside the city. I was now alone.

But this time, I decided to reinvent myself. The college was a fresh start, and no one knew who I was or what I had been through. It was the perfect opportunity to shed the old me—the heartbroken version—and embrace a new version of myself.

"New day, new me" became my mantra as soon as college started. I woke up early on the first day, ready to face the new chapter of my life. I wasn't particularly religious, but I did believe in God. My parents insisted I visit the Hanuman temple before going to college, so I did. Hanuman was my favourite deity—representing courage, strength, and loyalty—qualities that resonated deeply with me, as they do with many boys.

After visiting the temple and having breakfast, I headed straight to college. Little did I know, a huge surprise awaited me there. As I entered the campus, I scanned the surroundings, hoping to spot a familiar face. To my surprise, I saw one of my tuition mates sitting in the last row of the seminar hall. We weren't particularly close, but we were friendly, so I decided to sit with him.

A few minutes later, the principal gave a speech, and then we were free to mingle. The students in the last two rows began playing a game of truth or dare as an icebreaker, and my tuition mate introduced me to the others. As we played, I noticed a small figure sitting in the middle row. There was something about his posture, his body language, that seemed oddly familiar.

I stared for a moment, trying to place the feeling, and then, to my shock, he turned toward me. It was Anni. For a second, I couldn't believe my eyes. But it was him.

After we had drifted apart during high school, I had no idea he would be joining the same college. I quickly gestured for him to join us in the last row. He grabbed his bag and came over, and I introduced him to the group. It felt like a reunion of sorts. Anni quickly became part of the group, and we resumed playing the game.

The first day of college turned out better than I had anticipated. I had a friend by my side again. After college,

I went straight to Anni's house. I called my parents to let them know I'd be home by 8 p.m.

We took a walk around the park, and the first question Anni asked when we were alone was, *"Did you move on?"*

I looked at him and smiled.

"I know that smile. You haven't moved on, have you?" he asked, his tone teasing.

"I'm moving on now, in this college," I replied, trying to sound confident.

Anni already knew the story about the camp. I had called him right after it ended to update him.

"I don't think so," he said, giving me a knowing look.

"This time, I'm not alone. I have you," I said in a kind of bromantic way, trying to change the subject.

The conversation shifted, and though I still thought about Pari, I was determined to move on. I told myself I would start fresh the next day.

When I got home that evening, I couldn't help but smile. Seeing Anni again made me feel like I was taking a step forward. My mom noticed my happiness and asked, *"Happy to be classmates with Anni again?"*

"Yeah! I was worried about how I would make new friends, but seeing Anni again made me feel better," I replied.

My mom was happy for me. Parents just want their children to be happy, after all. But as I lay in bed that night, my thoughts inevitably turned to Pari.

I lay there, staring at the ceiling, the fan spinning slowly above me. I realized something: no matter how hard I tried, a part of me would always be stuck on her. Why? I wasn't sure. Maybe because she was the first person I truly loved, or maybe because she was the one who had hurt me the most. But no matter the reason, I knew I could never fully move on.

The next morning, I was woken up by the delicious smell of coffee in my mom's hand. She had pulled the blanket off me to wake me up. I felt refreshed and ready for the day ahead. After having coffee, I got ready and rushed to college.

That day, my mom dropped me off at college. We had a good routine going now. Classes were progressing, and on the fourth day of college, we were assigned to our sections. Anni got section A, and I was placed in section B. I was a little nervous at first, but we still shared most of the subjects, so it wasn't a big deal.

The days in college passed by quickly, and before I knew it, I was settling into a rhythm. It was lunch break one day, and I had already eaten when I noticed a book had fallen off a desk. I picked it up and saw the name "Advaya" written on the front page. It was a girl's name, and I didn't recognize it. I thought someone had mistakenly placed it on the wrong side of the room, so I put it on the podium.

A few minutes later, a girl came to retrieve the book. I didn't get a good look at her face, but something about her caught my attention. Little did I know, this would be the start of a new friendship. Advaya and her best friend, Sowmika, would soon become two of my closest friends.

It was a few months into college when we were practicing for an activity at one of our friend's houses. We weren't really practicing, just goofing off. Someone recorded the funny moments and posted them on Instagram. I reposted the story, and Advaya reacted with a laughing emoji. That was the first time we interacted, and somehow, that simple exchange led to us becoming friends.

The first year of pre-university passed by quickly, almost like a breeze. We were already on holiday when the pandemic hit. At first, it was just a 14-day lockdown, but soon it became clear that things were much worse than anyone had anticipated. Social distancing, masks, and endless rumours about the virus took over our lives.

Then came another surprise: Jai, who had been studying outside the city, came back home and joined the same college. Now, I had both of my best friends in the same college. When Jai first arrived, I introduced him to everyone, including Anni. The two of them hit it off, and our group grew even closer.

But just as things were settling into a new normal, the virus spread like wildfire, and the entire country went into lockdown. We were all confined to our homes, and what was supposed to be a 14-day break turned into an indefinite one.

At first, it was frustrating—nothing to do but sit at home and scroll through social media. But as time passed, we became more active online. Social media became our lifeline, and we kept in touch with each other through messaging and video calls. We played multiplayer games like *Among Us*, which kept us entertained during the long days.

The lockdown also brought its own challenges—online classes, online tests, and the constant uncertainty of the future. But as the months passed, we learned to adapt.

It was during this time that I started to realize something important: the future wasn't as important as the present. I had spent so much time chasing after the idea of moving on, of finding closure, of forgetting about Pari. But the truth was, I was never going to forget her.

I didn't need to forget her. I just needed to let go.

8

Simple Notifications...

It was the 28th of December, 2020, a day that began like any other, yet would soon become etched in my memory forever. I woke up at 11 a.m. My sleep schedule had been completely off the rails for the past few weeks, but it didn't bother me much. I grabbed my phone, checked a few notifications, and without a second thought, went to brush my teeth. I squeezed toothpaste onto my toothbrush and popped it into my mouth, all while scrolling through Instagram.

As I mindlessly swiped through my feed, I noticed a follow request notification. Without thinking, I clicked on it.

Suddenly, I froze. I nearly choked on the toothpaste I had just put in my mouth. My heart skipped a beat, and the sharp, spicy taste of the toothpaste made my throat burn as my eyes watered in shock. There, staring back at me from the notification, was the name I hadn't seen in years: *Pari.*

I couldn't believe it. This wasn't a dream. The paste in my mouth was proof enough. I was in shock, but also overwhelmed with a rush of joy. I had no idea why, but my heart raced, and I felt a surge of happiness I hadn't felt in ages.

I quickly accepted the follow request and sent her a request in return. I couldn't stop smiling. I felt like I was floating on air. That day, all the progress I had made in moving on from her seemed to vanish in an instant. The past few months of self-imposed healing went out the window. It was like a switch had been flipped, and suddenly, I was back to square one.

I went about my day, but the thought of her lingered in my mind. I went into the shower, phone in hand, obsessively refreshing her profile to see if she had accepted my request yet. I couldn't wait to see her pictures. I wanted to see her eyes again—those beautiful, dark eyes—and that smile that always made my heart skip a beat. It had been almost three years since I last saw her, and the anticipation was driving me crazy.

After getting dressed and ready for the day, I had breakfast—well, brunch, technically—around 12 p.m. I kept my phone in my room because I knew my mom would start yelling at me if she saw me holding my phone while eating. As soon as I finished, I rushed to check my phone, and there it was: she had accepted my request.

My excitement was through the roof. I couldn't wait any longer. I clicked on her profile, and there it was—her latest post. It had been uploaded just a day before, and the photo looked like it had been taken months ago, before the lockdown. It was from a flower show.

In the picture, the background was a sea of flowers in shades of pink, white, red, and beige. And there, standing at the left side of the frame, was Pari. She was wearing a simple dark blue top, and her smile—oh, that smile—was as beautiful as I remembered. The flowers in the background seemed to complement her beauty perfectly.

For a moment, I was completely lost in the picture. I felt like I was surrounded by the flowers, rolling in the petals, enveloped in the warmth of her presence. That one image made me realize something: no matter how much the world seemed to fall apart, I couldn't keep loving her selfishly. It wasn't fair to either of us. But every time I looked at her smile, I fell even harder.

Despite my feelings, I still lacked the courage to message her. So, I did the only thing I could think of—I liked her picture. It was a subtle way to let her know I had seen it, that I was paying attention. But I wasn't expecting any response.

A week went by, and I heard nothing. I began to think that maybe I had overestimated her interest. But then, after a month or so, something unexpected happened. She replied to one of my Instagram stories—a funny reel I had posted. She sent a laughing emoji.

My heart skipped a beat. I couldn't believe it. I quickly replied with a smiling emoji, unsure of what to say next. Then, a message from her appeared on my screen:

"How are you?"

I stared at the message for a moment, unsure of how to respond. I replied with a simple, *"I'm fine. And you?"*

Her response was quick. *"Yep. I'm fine too."*

And just like that, the conversation had started. I didn't know where it would go, but I was excited. She asked me about how the lockdown had been for me, and we exchanged a few more messages. It felt natural, easy, and before I knew it, ten minutes had passed.

That was the moment I felt a strange peace settle in my heart. It was like a weight had been lifted, and I could breathe easier. I didn't know why, but it felt nice to talk to her again.

The next morning, I woke up and checked my phone, half-expecting nothing. But to my surprise, there was a message from her: *"Good morning!"*

The moment I read it, I couldn't help but smile. My morning went from average to perfect in an instant. I replied quickly, and the conversation continued. She asked me if I had eaten breakfast yet.

It was around 11:30 a.m., and I had just woken up. I didn't want to admit that, so I lied and told her I had already had breakfast. But I couldn't help but feel guilty for lying. When I finally confessed, she laughed at my excuse, sending me a laughing emoji.

From that point on, our conversations became a daily routine. We exchanged good morning and good night texts, talked about the current situation, shared movie recommendations, and just caught up. It felt like old times, but different.

One day, out of the blue, she asked, *"Don't you use WhatsApp?"*

I was a little taken aback. *"Yes, I do,"* I replied.

She didn't hesitate for a second. *"Then give me your number. Chatting on Instagram is kind of hectic and boring, don't you think?"*

I was stunned. She had asked for my number so directly. It impressed me. It was bold, and I liked that about her. I gave her my number, and within minutes, my phone buzzed with a message from her on WhatsApp.

"Hi, from now on we'll chat here. Okay?"

I quickly replied, *"Okay."*

From that moment on, we switched to WhatsApp, and everything felt more personal. No distractions, just us talking. It was a new level of closeness. On Instagram, you could talk to anyone, but on WhatsApp, it felt more intimate. It was just the two of us, and that felt special.

We stopped chatting on Instagram, and our conversations became even more frequent. Every day, I felt like I was getting closer to her again. It was strange, almost surreal. But it was also exactly what I had been hoping for, even if I hadn't realized it at the time.

I was no longer just a person from her past. I was someone she was willing to talk to again, and that was enough for me.

One day, as I sat sipping my coffee and mindlessly scrolling through Facebook, a video caught my attention. It was about a dog up for adoption—a white and black Pomeranian puppy. The owners had abandoned it on a village road because it was a female puppy. The location listed was near my grandparents' house, about 10 to 15 kilometres away. My heart sank as I watched the video, and I immediately showed it to my grandfather, asking him if we could adopt the puppy and bring it home.

At first, my grandfather disagreed. We already had a dog, Sniper, a massive German Shepherd we had gotten to guard our farm. Sniper and I had spent countless hours together when he was a puppy, playing and bonding. As he grew older, he became a bit more reserved, though still friendly. He would bark at strangers or any other animals, but he had never been aggressive with me.

I tried to convince my grandfather, explaining that I could train Sniper not to harm the new puppy. After much pleading, he finally relented. I immediately called my grandparents and asked them to go and pick up the puppy. They agreed, and that same day, my grandfather went to get her. I couldn't wait to meet the little pup.

The next day, my dad and I decided to drive to my grandparents' house to pick up the puppy. It was during the lockdown, so travel was restricted, and private vehicles were stopped and asked for their reasons. But we knew of a backroad that passed through a village, free from checkpoints. My dad decided to take that route, and I eagerly joined him.

That night, as I was chatting with Pari, I told her about the puppy and how I was going to bring it home. She seemed genuinely interested and asked me to send her a picture once I had it. I told her there wouldn't be any network in the village, but I promised to send the picture as soon as I got home.

The next day, my dad and I made our way to my grandparents' house. I could barely contain my excitement. As soon as we arrived, I ran straight to the shed where the puppy was. She was curled up in a basket, chewing on a piece of dry grass she had found. My grandfather had already bathed her, and she looked clean and shiny, her black and white fur gleaming in the sunlight. He mentioned that she had been very thin and dirty when they first found her, but after some food and care, she was lively and playful.

We decided to name her Oreo, a fitting name for her black and white fur. After spending some time with her, my grandparents insisted that we stay with them for a few days due to the lockdown. I wasn't thrilled about the idea. While I loved visiting my grandparents, I was anxious to get home and talk to Pari. The village had no network coverage from my phone provider, and I knew I wouldn't be able to message her. I reluctantly agreed to stay.

The days at my grandparents' house felt like an eternity. I spent my time playing with Oreo and petting all the other animals, but without the constant stream of messages from Pari, I felt strangely empty. Each night, I would think about how I would text her as soon as I had a signal. But there was no way to reach her, and I couldn't help but feel guilty for not telling her about my sudden change of plans.

The fourth day arrived, and finally, my dad decided it was time to head home. I was eager to get Oreo back to our house and, more importantly, to get my phone back so I could message Pari. We packed up the puppy in a cardboard box, lined with a bedsheet for comfort, and began our journey back. The drive was uneventful, but I was too excited to focus on anything else.

Once we arrived home, I immediately ran to show my mom the puppy. She was hesitant at first, worried about the extra work that would come with taking care of another dog. But I knew, deep down, that within a day or two, both my parents would be doting on Oreo, just as they had done with Sniper.

I put Oreo in Sniper's old cage for the time being, knowing that introducing them would take some time. I had to train Sniper not to harm her, and I would need to take Oreo to the vet for her vaccinations. But that could wait for another day.

First, I needed to check my phone. It had been off for the past few days because I had forgotten to bring my charger, and my grandparents didn't have the right cable. I quickly grabbed the charger, plugged it in, and waited for my phone to turn on. As soon as it did, a flood of notifications came through, and I saw five messages from Pari. I had expected maybe one, but five?

The first message was from the morning I left: "Good morning." Then, a few hours later, "Still not home?" and a sad emoji. Two days after that, "Where are you?" with another sad emoji.

I felt a pang of guilt for not updating her sooner, but I quickly replied, "Hi, I'm back!" Almost immediately, she responded, asking where I had been. I explained that we had decided to stay at my grandparents' for a few extra days. I also sent her a photo of Oreo, and she immediately praised the puppy, calling her cute and commenting on her big puppy eyes.

We spent the next several minutes chatting about Oreo, her playful antics, and how adorable she was. As I chatted with Pari, I felt a warmth in my chest. She was so kind and caring, and I realized that I had missed our conversations more than I had let myself admit. She was a pet lover, and she seemed genuinely happy for me and the new addition to our family.

That evening, I took Oreo to the vet for her vaccinations and bought her some toys. I spent the rest of the day helping Oreo settle in and trying to train Sniper to get along with her. But no matter how busy I was, I couldn't shake the thought of Pari.

Later that night, after dinner, I grabbed my phone and texted Pari. We started talking again, and she mentioned how empty WhatsApp had felt without my texts for those five days. It made me realize that she wasn't just texting me out of boredom—she genuinely wanted to talk. That realization hit me hard. I had always thought I was the only one feeling this way, but she was missing me too.

I didn't know how to respond, so I just sent an emoji. But deep down, I knew that I was falling for her even harder. She was the one for me, but I still couldn't shake the fear of confessing my feelings. If I told her how I felt, I risked losing the friendship we had worked so hard to build.

But after we started talking on the phone, I began to sense something more. There was a vibe between us, something unspoken but undeniable. I couldn't help but wonder if maybe, just maybe, she felt the same way.

But then doubt crept in. Was I just imagining things? Was I being delusional? Or was there something more to our connection than I was willing to admit? I didn't know the answer, but I couldn't shake the feeling that something was changing between us.

And so, I continued to hold back, unsure of what to do. But one thing was certain: every day, I felt closer to Pari, and the more we talked, the harder it became to ignore the feelings growing inside me.

9

Words of a Wanderer...

One random day, I decided to catch up with one of my close friends, Sai. We met around two in the afternoon, had lunch together, and as we were about to leave, I bought a coffee to take along for the walk.

As we strolled down the street, we encountered a homeless man. His dishevelled appearance and the distant look in his eyes suggested he was mentally unstable. He approached us and asked for something. I checked my wallet but realized I didn't have any cash. Sai, however, pulled out a fifty-rupee note and offered it to him. To our surprise, the man refused the money and instead asked for food. I told him to take the money and buy food, but he insisted, saying, "Hotels won't allow me inside. Please, just get me something to eat."

It struck me deeply—here was a man who wasn't asking for money, but for something more fundamental. He was hungry. I quickly walked to the nearby hotel and ordered food for him. When I handed it over, he thanked us and asked what we did for a living.

Sai, always the curious one, asked, "Where do you live?"

The man pointed toward an under-construction building nearby. "I've been living there for the past three months," he said.

I asked him, "Don't they ask you to leave?"

"No," he replied, "they don't bother me."

Then Sai, in his usual inquisitive way, asked, "What about your family?"

The man's face softened, and a shadow passed over his eyes. "My wife died three years ago from cancer," he said quietly. "I lost everything that day. My wife, my everything."

We both fell silent. It was a moment of heavy sadness that hung between us. But Sai, wanting to know more, asked, "What happened after that?"

The man looked away, his voice cracking with emotion. "I loved her so much. She was my everything. But I lost her. And I cursed God for taking her away from me. What did I ask for? A paradise? No. I just asked Him to save her. What was it to Him? Nothing. But I lost everything. What kind of God is He? If He were real, He would have saved her."

The rawness of his words hit me like a slap. I felt my hands shake and my heart race. My eyes welled up as I tried to process what he had said. His pain was real, undeniable. Despite his appearance, this man had known love in its purest form, and he had lost it. The grief he felt was something only he could understand, and in that moment, I realized how powerful love could be.

That evening, back at home, I sat in my room holding my coffee, my mind replaying the words of that stranger. I knew, deep down, that Pari was the one I wanted in my life. No one else. I loved her more than I could express, but fear gripped me. I was terrified of confessing my feelings to her. I had already lost her once before, and I wasn't sure I could bear to lose her again. But after hearing the man's story, I realized that time waits for no one. I couldn't wait forever, because one day, the opportunity might slip away.

I had been so afraid of confessing, of the consequences, of ruining our friendship. But in that moment, I knew that I had to act before it was too late. Love, like the man's, is fleeting, and if you don't seize it when you have the chance, it might be gone forever.

I sat with my phone in hand, trying to figure out how to express everything I was feeling. But no words seemed right. Then, after a long pause, I gathered the courage and texted Pari, "What am I to you?"

As soon as I hit send, my heart pounded in my chest. I felt a knot form in my stomach, and I began to second-guess myself. What if I ruined everything? What if she didn't feel the same way?

A few moments later, I saw the dreaded "typing" notification. My mind raced, and I wondered if I had made a huge mistake. Then, her reply came through: "You're my best friend. Am I not your best friend?"

I let out a breath I didn't realize I was holding. She took my question as a joke and started teasing me, pulling my leg as usual. I felt a wave of relief wash over me, and I joined in on the playful banter. We laughed for hours, the conversation stretching late into the night, and finally, we wished each other goodnight before falling asleep.

The next morning, I woke up later than usual. Pari had already sent me a good morning message, and I replied as I went about my morning routine. After brushing my teeth and grabbing my coffee, I checked my phone and saw a message from her: "You know what?"

Curious, I called her up. She answered with a laugh in her voice, and I asked, "What's up? What do you mean by that?"

She giggled. "You came into my dream last night."

I couldn't help but smile. "Really? What happened in the dream?"

She laughed even harder. "It was so weird! You were still in 9th grade, but I was older. And for some reason, I was beating you up. I don't know why, but it was so funny!"

I couldn't stop laughing either. "Beating me up, huh? I don't know why I was so young, but I guess it makes sense since we last talked when I was in high school."

She continued to laugh. "Yeah, but beating you felt kind of good," she teased.

We laughed together, and I felt a warmth in my chest. It was clear that we had grown closer, and I couldn't deny that I was happy to be in her thoughts. But there was still a part of me that wondered how she truly felt about me. I had started to feel like we were in a relationship, but I wasn't sure if she felt the same way. My heart said yes, but my mind hesitated.

One day, as we were talking, Pari mentioned that Sam from school had texted her on Instagram. She said they had talked that morning. I felt a pang of jealousy twist in my chest. Sam had always liked her, and I knew he had a way with words. He was confident, charming, and could flirt with anyone. I wondered if she was starting to like him instead of me.

But despite my insecurities, Pari continued to talk to me the same way she always had. She called me regularly, texted me constantly, and never gave Sam as much attention as she did me. My fears started to fade, replaced by the hope that maybe, just maybe, she felt something for me too.

Days passed, and our bond grew stronger. I had started to realize that, despite all the uncertainties, she had become a constant in my life. And maybe, just maybe, I was the same to her

One evening, as I was talking to Pari over a phone call, I casually asked, "Didn't Sam message you?"

She replied, "Yes, he messaged me this morning."

"Why didn't you reply?" I asked, curious.

There was a brief silence before she answered, her tone laced with irritation, "Because you're my best friend, not him."

Hearing those words, my heart swelled with happiness. Her words felt like a reassurance, a subtle reminder of the bond we shared.

Later that night, we continued our conversation over text. However, I noticed her replies were unusually slow. Concerned, I asked, "Are you sleepy? It's already 10:30."

"No," she replied. "I'm just filling out something called a digital autograph."

"A digital autograph?" I asked, puzzled.

After a minute, she texted again. "I'm back now."

Curious, I asked her about the autograph. She explained that Sam had sent her a forwarded message with questions to fill out, and she had just completed it. Jealousy bubbled up inside me again, but I kept my tone neutral. "Oh, is that so?"

To my surprise, she sent me the same forwarded message. "Fill this out," she insisted. "It'll be fun! We can exchange our answers."

At first, I wasn't interested in such things, but Pari had a way of convincing me with her playful charm. "Come on, it'll be fun!" she said, her words laced with that irresistible cuteness. I couldn't say no.

The message contained eight questions:

1. Your name
2. Date of birth
3. Favourite colour
4. Favourite food
5. Favourite sport
6. What am I to you?
7. Best friend
8. Your crush

I started filling it out. I answered the first five questions easily: my name, date of birth, and all my favourites. For the sixth question, "What am I to you?" I wrote, *best friend*. For the seventh, "Best friend," I wrote, *Pari*.

But when I reached the eighth question, "Your crush," I froze. My heart screamed to write her name, but my courage faltered. I ended up typing *none* and sent the completed form back to her.

Pari also sent me her answers. Her responses read:

- Name: Pari
- Date of birth: 21/05
- Favourite colour: Black
- Favourite food: Ice cream
- Favourite sports: Volleyball, Cricket
- What am I to you: Best friend
- Best friend: You
- Your crush: ....

The line of dots at the end of her last answer caught my attention immediately. I couldn't help but ask, "What does that mean?"

She replied with a smiling emoji and said, "Nothing."

But my heart sank. I couldn't help but think she had someone else in mind, and that those dots represented a name she didn't want to share. I pressed her for an answer, asking repeatedly, "What does it mean?"

After about thirty minutes of back-and-forth, she finally replied, "If I tell you, you might feel bad."

My heart started racing. I tried to remain calm, though my thoughts were spiraling. "Just tell me," I said softly.

She hesitated, and I saw the dreaded "typing" notification linger for what felt like an eternity. Then her message finally came through:

"I don't know how to tell you this, but I think I'm starting to like you. I love talking to you. The way you make me feel special and happy—it's something I've never felt before. I think I've been developing feelings for you ever since we started talking on phone calls. Before that, when you went to your grandparents' house, I felt like something was missing, but I didn't realize it was you. After we started talking again, I understood. I wanted to tell you earlier, but I was scared of ruining our friendship, so I kept it to myself."

I froze. I got out of bed, my hands trembling as I read the message over and over again, just to make sure I wasn't imagining it. Tears welled up in my eyes. It felt like I had won something I had been longing for my entire life.

Still in disbelief, I replied with a single word: "Really?"

Pari responded, "Yes."

I felt a surge of emotions—joy, relief, and an overwhelming urge to tell her how I felt. But at that moment, all I could manage was, "I like you too."

"Really?" she asked, mirroring my earlier reply.

We both paused, as if processing the magnitude of what had just happened.

"Yes," I said. "I've liked you since the 7th grade."

"Really?" she asked again, her tone filled with surprise.

"Yes," I admitted. "That's why I didn't talk to you much during the NCC camp. I was scared of making a fool of myself."

"You should have told me when we started talking again!" she said.

"I was afraid of ruining our friendship," I confessed.

She laughed softly. "So, let me get this straight. We both liked each other but didn't confess because we were scared of ruining our friendship?"

"Not exactly," I replied. "You liked me for three months and didn't confess. I liked you for almost six years and didn't confess."

"You're such an idiot," she said, laughing.

From that night onward, I became her "loving idiot," and she became my everything.

Sometimes, failure isn't the end—it's just the beginning of something beautiful. If your love is true, it will always find its way back to you.

ᘓᘓᘓ

And so, as the final petal of uncertainty fell, their love bloomed brighter than ever—a testament to patience, resilience, and the quiet courage of a heart that never stopped believing.

Seven years of longing, quiet hope, and unwavering devotion culminated in a moment that felt as if the universe had conspired to align their souls. When she finally looked into his eyes and confessed what he had longed to hear, the world seemed to stand still. Her words, soft yet powerful, broke through the barriers of doubt and hesitation, setting their hearts free.

It wasn't just a confession; it was a beginning. A beginning for two souls who had waited too long to find their way back to each other. The journey was anything but easy. He had weathered the storms of uncertainty, the ache of unspoken feelings, and the fear that perhaps she might never feel the same. But love—true love—has a way of prevailing.

For her, it wasn't just about discovering her feelings; it was about finding the courage to trust in them, to let herself be vulnerable, and to believe in the boy who had loved her through it all. His steadfastness wasn't just a testament to his love but a mirror that reflected her own heart, making her see what had been there all along.

As they walked hand in hand, stepping into a future built on years of hope and unspoken dreams, it was clear that their love wasn't new. It was rebloomed—stronger, deeper, and more enduring than they could have ever imagined.

To the readers who believe in love that endures time and trials: may Rebloomed Love remind you that love, no matter how long it takes, will find its way when it's meant to. Hold onto hope, nurture your heart, and never stop believing in the magic of a love that's written in the stars.

And so, their love story reached its long-awaited crescendo, a union seven years in the making. Her confession had been his dream, and together they built a world full of hope and promises, basking in the joy of a love that had finally blossomed. Yet, as the final pages closed, a shadow lingered—an unspoken question, an unease that neither could name.

Fate, it seemed, was not finished with them. What could tear apart two souls so deeply intertwined? What storm loomed on the horizon to challenge a love that had endured so much? The answers wait in the next chapter of their journey, where truths will unravel, hearts will be tested, and the unbreakable bond of their red thread will face its greatest trial.

Their story isn't over—it's only just beginning.

With love,

Tharun........